# Deadly Loyalties

Theytus Books

Library and Archives Canada Cataloguing in Publication

Storm, Jennifer, 1986-
Deadly loyalties / by Jennifer Storm.

ISBN 978-1-894778-39-8

I. Title.

PS8637.T675D42 2007    jC813'.6    C2007-905407-2

Printed on Ancient Forest Friendly
100% post consumer fibre paper.

Cover photo: Kailene Ramage

Author photo: Courtesy of Stephanie JM Photography

Designed by Suzanne Bates

Theytus Books
Penticton, B.C.

Printed and bound in Canada.

*On behalf on Theytus Books, we would like to acknowledge the support of the following:*

*We acknowledge the financial support of the Government of Canada through the Book Publishing Industry Development Program (BPIDP) for our publishing activities. We acknowledge the support of the Canada Council for the Arts which last year invested $20.1 million in writing and publishing throughout Canada. Nous remercions de son soutien le Conseil des Arts du Canada, qui a investi 20,1 millions de dollars l'an dernier dans les lettres et l'édition à travers le Canada. We acknowledge the support of the Province of British Columbia through the British Columbia Arts Council.*

 BRITISH COLUMBIA ARTS COUNCIL

 Canada Council for the Arts    Conseil des Arts du Canada

 Patrimoine canadien    Canadian Heritage

# Deadly Loyalties

Jennifer Storm

# Contents

# CHAPTER 1

My COTTON-DRY MOUTH WAS what woke me up. I sat up and felt bile creeping up my throat. The taste of last night's cigarettes and cheap beer starting to crawl upward. I shot out of bed and into the bathroom where I kept my head in the toilet, retching up all of last night. I tried bargaining with God, as I always do when I throw up, "God, if you exist, I promise I will believe in you forever and ever if you just make this puking stop. Oh man, I will never drink again." God never made the puking stop fast enough to prove himself to me.

I heard my mom banging on the door. "Are you sick, Blaise?"

I wiped the sides of my mouth with tissue paper. "Yeah, I'm coming down with something I think."

"It kinda smells like booze…" she pointed out.

I rolled my eyes at her behind the safety of a closed door.

"Well it's not. I'm just sick. Go away!"

I heard her footsteps going back up the stairs. I looked in the mirror while I turned the tap on. My hair was the same as it always was: long, dark and straight. I was so pale it would be hard to guess that I am actually Native. I wished I had darker skin. My face was shiny with sweat and my eyeliner was smudged in a way that made me look like I was crying. Was I crying last night? Wouldn't make sense. There was a mystery bruise on my knee –not the first time. That could've happened any time last night.

I rinsed out my mouth a couple of times so I wouldn't get my toothbrush all gross. Then I washed my face with my mom's decorative towel. She hated it when I used her decorative towels, but I thought it was stupid not to.

When I got upstairs my mom was chipper and chatting with her new boyfriend, who had slept over. I hated it when she brought them over without letting me know. They always tried to make friends with me and this morning was not a good time for that.

"Hey, Blaise, I heard you were sick?" He sat at our breakfast table, wearing sweats and an old t-shirt. His name slipped my mind, even though he had been around for awhile–longer than some of the others.

"Yeah," I said.

I looked to my mother, who was busy buttering his toast to go with his coffee.

"Blaise, why don't you go out and grab me the paper, honey?" my mom said.

I put my head in the fridge and made a disgusted face. She never called me honey, and she only acted like this when she was trying to sell someone the image of us being a happy, functional family. I grabbed a bottle of juice and closed the fridge door.

"You guys aren't doing anything. Why don't you get the paper? I don't even read the paper, so why would I want to go get it?"

I saw a glimpse of anger rise in my mom's eyes for a moment, then she turned and smiled at her boyfriend.

"She must be really sick. She usually loves going outside." She explained, trying to cover up my unattractive attitude.

"Yeah, to get the fuck away from here…" I mumbled under my breath.

"What was that?" she asked.

"I didn't say anything!" I said, heading back downstairs to my room.

Once in my room, I fought the urge to crawl back into bed. I had to get out of here before those annoying assholes upstairs tried to lecture me or talk to me. I put on my essential makeup: foundation, eyeliner, mascara and gloss. I put on some old sweater and jeans, put my hair in a pony-tail and went upstairs to the front door. Before I could get my second shoe on I heard my mother's voice calling.

"Blaise? Where are you going? I thought you were sick?"

*Damn it.*

I went back into the kitchen. She had an expression on her face, trying to look like she cared that I was sick. She didn't care. She just wanted me to stay home and warm up to her asshole boyfriend.

"I'm going over to Tom's place for a bit. I feel a bit better now." I faked a smile.

"I'll see you later," I said as I left.

Heading down the walkway, I immediately regretted not grabbing sunglasses, but did not want to go back in and risk getting cornered and told to stay in bed. The brightness of the sun was almost blinding and for a block or so I was shielding my eyes with my hands. My head was pounding.

Tom's place on Redwood avenue was only a couple of blocks from where I lived. Winnipeg during the day was not what it looked like at night. In this area, the night made everywhere seem like a dark back alley—a place not to be.

It seemed every time my mom and I moved we were getting closer to the worst parts of town—and now we were here. The streets were littered with stains that never came clean. Every smudge was like a hieroglyphic left behind to tell about what may have happened there.

When I reached Tom's house, he answered the door without his shirt. I tried to keep my face from giving away my surprise of seeing his skinny, half-naked body.

"Blaise, it's only noon! Why did you come over so goddamn early?"

"Because my mom and her loser boyfriend were annoying me." Tom just stared at me. Then he told me to come in and wait on the couch.

"Do you mind if I have a smoke?" I asked.

"Go ahead, my parents won't be home for awhile." Tom answered. The tv was on. "The View" was going to a commercial.

"So," I started, lighting my smoke, "how's it going?"

"Same ol' shit I guess. I was up 'til three in the morning last night, helping clean up my Mom's mess."

I looked around the living room; it looked the same to me, maybe just a little emptier. I was used to hearing about Tom's parents and their big fights. Only this time Tom's mother smashed all the breakable stuff, which was probably the most expensive.

I took a drag from my cigarette and stared at the television. I leaned back into the couch The room had a heavy, dreary darkness to it that felt comforting at the time. Faint light came through the living room window that turned the smoke from my cigarette into a dancing mirage. I imagined myself getting up off the couch and running my hand through the curtain of smoke; then I thought about getting high.

Tom had gone to his room to get dressed.

"Light up a joint, Tom!" I yelled.

A grunt came from the bedroom, then I heard, "Got none."

Tom came out wearing his favorite grey shirt, which was about two sizes too big, and he wore it almost every day. I remember he wore it on the first day of grade nine–the year we met. In the hallways it made him almost invisible. I knew he was a social leper since that first day I saw him. He would hit all the lockers as he walked by, scanning the other kids for eye contact. He'd say, 'hello/hey,' to any familiar face, but didn't seem to realize they never said it back. When the day came that he recognized me from math class, I was different and said, 'hey,' back.

It was obvious when Tom started putting his shoes on that we were going to go to Sheldon's house. Tom always wanted to hang out with Sheldon. I got off the couch and ran my fingers through the curtain of smoke before following him out the door.

Tom always told bullshit stories to Sheldon. When we got to Sheldon's place, the first thing Tom started talking about was how he almost got into a fight at school last Friday.

"The guy was talking all big, saying I was trying to steal his girlfriend. So I said 'if I wanted your girlfriend I woulda had her by now!' Ooh, you shoulda seen the look on his face, man."

Sheldon was in a gang. I never got to meet any of his gang members, but I never doubted that they existed. Sheldon had been my friend longer than anyone else. Our parents worked together at the hospital and took turns babysitting us when we were too young to stay home alone. We never really had much in common, but we were good friends. You could say he was a bad influence. He introduced me to everything wrong. He convinced me to skip school for the first time and to smoke my first joint. He also convinced me that pink corduroys weren't cool and that they made me look like a kid–no kid wants to hear that they look like a kid.

Knowing him as long as I have made us seem more like siblings or cousins. But if I were meeting him for the first time I'd probably mumble jokes, say really embarrassing things and get butterflies in my stomach. One time he told me I was beautiful. We were drunk and I was lying on the floor laughing because we tripped over each other while fighting for the bathroom. I didn't even need to go; I just wanted to be close to him.

We always hung out in Sheldon's room, even when his parents weren't home. His room smelt like wet clothes and pot. He had the entire unfinished basement as his bedroom. Tom and I were all jealous even though it was a scary looking room. I knew I could never sleep there. There were too many dark corners and hiding spots.

Tom was skipping through Sheldon's cd's and finally decided on a song I never heard before. I laid on the bed and saw a smoke curtain forming again by Sheldon's window. I imagined how I'd look if I swayed in it, twirling in one of those fancy skirts that make a pretty flower shape when you spin in them. I imagined myself twirling in it and the smoke dancing around me like it was my aura and my hair would look soft and dreamy, like it was under water. I imagined what it would be like to have butterflies in my belly.

"Sheldon? Do you have anything to eat?" Tom asked.

"Yeah, get me something too." I added.

"Why don't you guys get it yourselves?"

"Because we're the guests." I said, trying to smile as cute as I could.

Sheldon looked at me and headed upstairs to the kitchen.

"Yeah, yeah," he said.

I sat on the bed with Tom, who was already watching tv. We started watching a program about facelifts. Seeing people getting facelifts on tv made me second guess their reality. I couldn't understand why people would want to look younger if they were already old and married. I really thought the desire to be sexy was only for a certain age group. That sex was a dirty secret that was only seldom indulged. I always knew my logic was somehow off and that if someday someone was able to read my thoughts, they'd laugh at how young I was. I pulled out my cigarette, since there was nothing else to do. I lit it just as Sheldon was walking in with chocolate pudding.

"Hey, do you even have an ashtray for that?" Sheldon gestured to my cigarette.

"Yeah, don't worry, I'm using this." I told him, and pointed to the cup on the nightstand.

"Okay, here's your pudding then."

I put the pudding aside to finish my smoke. My stomach grumbled with hunger. The morning's queasiness had subsided. Dropping my cigarette butt into the cup-ashtray, I swirled it around in the few drops of liquid until it fizzled out.

Hearing someone enter the house, we all turned to look as Damion walked in the room.

"Hey, Blaise," Damion said.

"Yo, Damion!" Tom yelled.

Damion turned to Tom. They both did this weird high-five handshake. I assumed it was a guy thing because no one ever did it with me. Damion was Sheldon's best friend (besides me). They did almost everything together. Damion was hot in a way that was intimidating to me. He was always nice to me, was really good-looking and always had tons of girls after him. He's had lots of girlfriends, some of them not all that great either, but still, I felt he was always out of my league. I never really had the chance to have a crush on him. Every time I tried to imagine kissing him, he would always outshine me and I couldn't stand it. Even my imagination knew he was too perfect to be with me.

Damion and Sheldon had this way of communicating without speaking. Even though both Tom and I knew they were communicating, we could never completely figure out what they were talking about. We could only guess. When Sheldon suggested we go to the store, I knew what he and Damion had in mind. They wanted to meet up with their dealer.

Sheldon would never admit to me that he was buying drugs off someone behind my back. He always treated me and Tom like we were kids even though we were only two years younger than him and Damion. I was the second youngest of the five of us. At fourteen years old I was in grade nine. Tom was the youngest. He was fourteen too, but I beat him by five months. He was in his second year of grade eight. Sheldon and Damion were both sixteen, and both high-school dropouts.

On the way to the store, we ended up talking about a huge party down town at this guy Randy's house. He was Damion and Sheldon's age. Damion was saying how Randy told him to bring as many people as he wanted, preferably girls. I felt my heart thump twice, the way it does when you go to your first dance. This would be my first real high school party. I didn't want to seem excited, because that would be lame. I pulled out my lighter and started sparking it repetitively.

"Do you want to come? It's next Saturday." Damion asked.

"I might go. It all depends." I answered, trying to be cool.

"Well, you could bring some of your other friends. The more that come the better."

I thought about inviting the friends I had, but they were all losers compared to kids in higher grades. It would be embarrassing. All I could think of was them sitting at the party giggling amongst themselves and talking about boys they'd never talk to. I didn't want to be associated with them at my first big break for popularity.

"Well?" Damion asked hopefully.

"I'll see if anyone wants to come," I lied.

When we got to the store Damion made his way to the candy section with Sheldon. And just as I predicted, Tom followed me to the pop cooler. The shopkeeper shifted her eyes back and forth from us to other customers. I looked through all the brands until I found our favorite; Pepsi. I took out a two litre bottle and walked up to the cash register. Damion and Sheldon had already disappeared. They were outside and around a corner, doing their secret business with the mystery dealer.

After I bought my pop, I stepped outside to wait for them with Tom. When they met us outside the front of the store they told us some bullshit story about how they both had to go to the bathroom and couldn't wait. They did, however, have about five dollars worth of candy in their pockets. I asked them if they had a Wonder Bar for me, and of course, they did. I took the bar away from Sheldon and devoured it. Tom shared some five cent candies with Sheldon and I suddenly felt really special getting a chocolate bar all to myself.

# CHAPTER 2

AT SCHOOL THE FOLLOWING WEEK when the bell rang ending the first period, I went outside for a smoke . Carly was outside smoking, too. We had been smoke buddies since the beginning of the school year. We met on a rainy day because she was standing under the umbrella her mom made her bring to school. I'll never forget the peachy perfume she wore; it smelt cheap and sexy at the same time.

Carly had heard about the party I was going to. She asked me what I was going to wear. I knew she was fishing for an invitation. I had told some girls that I was going but that I wasn't allowed to bring anyone.

"I dunno what I'll wear. Normal clothes I guess." I said, blowing smoke rings into the air.

"Well, just make sure you don't wear anything too sexy, cause then all the other girls will start giving you dirty looks and guys might think you're a slut. Don't be too laid back either, cause then guys won't think you're hot and girls will think you're lame."

Carly always slicked her hair into a tight ponytail that was completely stiff with gel. She was only giving me fashion advise to bring up the party. The second bell rang and I changed the subject.

"I gotta go, Carly. Maybe I'll see you at lunch." Carly rolled her eyes at me, annoyed that I wouldn't invite her to come to the party with me.

I headed back into the school. The day had been going by slowly. I had a double math class with the most boring teacher in school, followed by gym. If they made my schedule so that gym was before those math classes I probably wouldn't be failing gym. Why make it so tempting to skip?

Sheldon's house was walking distance from school, but the chances of him being there were slim. I didn't want to run into his mom and have her tell on me for leaving school early. She'd probably say something like, "When Sheldon's back in school you best believe that he wouldn't get away with it either." But, I decided to check Sheldon anyways, and if he wasn't home, then I'd go back to school. I grabbed my jacket and left the school. I walked quickly until the school grounds were out of sight. When walking, I'd play a game where I would count candy wrappers on my way to places. A patch of sidewalk reflected little diamonds of shattered glass. It looked like a star exploded last night and all its stardust fell quietly and unnoticed. I saw an old Kit Kat wrapper. 'One'. Then a Labbatt's bottle wrapper still attached to a shard of glass–'Doesn't count'.

When I reached Sheldon's street, I could see him on his porch. I figured that he was likely having a cigarette and that would mean his mom was probably home. She didn't like us smoking in the house. I picked up my pace with my hands in my pockets and my head up, forgetting my wrapper counting. As I walked up his driveway I realized he was smoking a joint. He looked at me with a smile and said,

"You skippin again, little girl?" he knew I hated it when he called me that.

"Share?" I asked, realizing his mom must not be home after all.

He shrugged his shoulders, still smiling. He looked to the other end of the street and took another hoot. He passed it to me without even looking my way. His smile faded suddenly.

"Oh fuck! Quick, Blaise, get in the house!" Sheldon said with his eyes fixed down the street toward three figures heading our way.

I looked at him confused, "What? Why? What about this?" I said holding the joint up to him. He grabbed it and threw it over the porch. Grabbing my arm, he shoved me hard towards the door. Then I knew he was serious, so I did as he said.

Turning off the living room light, I perched on the couch by the front window. I had a bad feeling, but I just sat there, quiet, and opened the curtain slightly. Sheldon looked angry, not open and friendly as he usually looked. He was shouting at one of the approaching guys. From inside the house I couldn't translate the muffled sound. I peered closer to see who he was yelling at. There were three guys approaching the house who looked to be around nineteen or twenty-years-old.

When they reached the front yard, they stood on the lawn gesturing for Sheldon to come down off the porch. One was a really fat looking Native guy. The other two were black. They all looked scary to me — tough and mean. Clearly not Sheldon's friends. Sheldon shifted his weight anxiously. I wondered if he was scared.

Sitting on my knees on the couch, I made sure to keep my head low and not to be seen. I didn't move for fifteen minutes. My stomach was tensed and my jaw clenched tight. I could feel the tension outside as the level of anger seemed to increase. Sheldon remained on the porch. Every now and then the guys on the lawn would show off their weapons, I guessed as a token of their seriousness. The Native guy flipped his switchblade open and closed over and over again. I wondered if I should go out there and help Sheldon, but how? What could I do? I was no threat to the three men. I could threaten to call the police, but Sheldon would ream me out for doing something so stupid.

The shouting from outside worsened. I felt I couldn't sit there any longer. But just as I was about to get up, Sheldon jumped down off the porch onto the front lawn, slowly approaching the guys until they were face to face. I stayed where I was, glued to the couch.

It looked like Sheldon was telling them to leave. He was gesturing with his arms. I could hear him swearing, and then he reached one hand behind his back. One of the black guys jumped on Sheldon and pushed him to the ground. Then the big Native guy started throwing punches down on Sheldon. The big guy moved and blocked my view so I couldn't see Sheldon. I wanted to get up and go outside to stop the fight. But what could I do? I couldn't make these guys stop. And Sheldon would get so pissed off if I interfered in one of his fights. Going outside would do nothing but get my own ass kicked.

Dread and fear crept through my body as the fight worsened and the only one getting beat was Sheldon. I couldn't get up. Hypnotized, I couldn't move. I caught a glimpse of Sheldon; his hands were all bloody and so was his face. He was down on the ground getting hit from all sides.

My brain was like television static. I was frozen and covered in electric snow. I imagined I was throwing myself at the window, banging my fists against the glass to scare them off. All I could see were glimpses of Sheldon's sweater flailing like it was caught in some sort of heavy tornado. The big guy took out a knife and reached down near Sheldon's face. He pierced the switch deep into Sheldon's throat. Covering my mouth, I inhaled a scream. Then I saw calm. The big guy tore the switchblade out of Sheldon. They all stood up and glanced around the street. I ducked lower. Two of them started to run off. They looked back at their buddy who was standing over Sheldon. "Hurry up, let's go," they must have called to him, because he snapped out of it and started to run too.

My hands trembled. It took about three seconds for me to blink again and then stand up. I ran to the door but then stopped. I didn't want those thugs to see me. I had seen them and I didn't want them to know that. I waited and watched until they disappeared down the street before I cautiously opened the door.

I stepped onto the porch and ran forward. I crashed into the railing, my hands gripping the splintering wood. As I neared Sheldon, my heart started beating upwards, hard and fast towards my throat. He was sprawled motionless on the ground. Blood formed a puddle around him. His hand was on his neck, blood oozing from between his fingers. I approached his motionless body on the ground. I wanted to cry, but instead I had to fight against vomiting. It felt like every organ in my body was misplaced. I didn't know what to do. My body was no longer frozen, but my mind was. I felt nothing, like it wasn't happening.

I shook my head, then quickly turned and went back into the house to the phone. I dialed 911. An operator answered and asked for my emergency.

"Umm. My friend just got stabbed in the neck. Three men were in on it!" I said, finally starting to cry. "I saw it all happen!"

"What's the address?" The operator asked. I paused, "Uhhh, I-I-I can't remember!....on Phillips street, near the high school." I threw in a bit of cussing in my annoyance. Why wasn't my brain working? And why couldn't the operator just figure it out? "Just get here fast! Don't you guys trace these calls? Just hurry. And bring an ambulance or something!" I yelled, and hung up the phone.

I ran back outside to see Sheldon. His chest wasn't moving. I didn't even know why I asked for an ambulance when I knew he was already dead. I sat down on the grass beside him. *Maybe I shouldn't stay here,* I thought. *Who knows what the police will think?* I looked over at Sheldon. His eyes were half open so I closed them. He wouldn't want anyone to see him like that. I reached into his pocket and found a couple grams of weed and fifty dollars. His black date book was in his other pocket. Sheldon's switchblade lay on the ground, bloodstained from retaliation. I grabbed his weed and switch so no one would stereotype him as some troublemaking kid that was just asking for it. I had to hide this stuff fast. I got off the ground and ran toward the bus stop. I was shaking and crying and out of breath. I wiped my face and tried to compose myself before the bus came. I had to get downtown, fast.

I knew Damion was probably at the pool hall bar, so as soon as it was in sight I pulled the cord. The driver stopped right in front of the pool hall. *You'd better be here, Damion,*

I thought. As I walked into the pool hall I could see right across to the bar where he stood with some blonde–as usual.

This bar was infamously known to local teens as the place that doesn't card. Only a few kids got kicked out for not having ID. I never went in before because I didn't know how I'd take it if I was one of those kids. My friends would never let me live it down.

He looked at me and waved me over. I caught sight of my wet, pale face in the mirrored wall as I walked up to him. He looked at me carefully.

"Hey, what's wrong?"

"We need to talk." I said, and asked him to sit down with me, leaving the blonde at the bar.

I never thought I would ever be a person to have to break news about death. I never thought I would be the kind of person who would have a dead friend, either. I wanted to cry but felt frustratingly numb. I wondered how long it would take my heart to figure out Sheldon was never gonna come back.

"Sheldon's dead."

He looked at me, taking a moment to register my seriousness.

"Sheldon?" he asked.

I nodded at him, "I saw it all." A tear fell.

"I called 911 and left with his weed and switch. Then I came down here as fast as I could. I didn't know what to do. Do you think I should go back there and talk to them?" I asked.

Damion took my hand and walked me outside. He hung his head down and kept shaking it back and forth, no, no. We walked for a bit and I tried to comfort him. This was our first serious moment together.

He led me to a shabby old building. "We'll hang at my father's house until I figure something out," he said. As I followed him up to the building I took a mental note: Damion didn't have a dad, he had a father.

When we reached his building and went inside, we walked up a long flight of stairs. The walls were cracked and the ceiling was water-stained. There was old wallpaper with little pink flowers poking through greasy fingerprints and years of grime. It felt like forever walking up those stairs.

When we made it to the apartment, Damion guided me right to his room.

"Lay down for a bit, you probably need to rest," he said, coaxing me down on his bed. I did as he told me, and he sat down on the chair and rested his head in his hands. I looked at him. *Did he see me staring?* He was biting the inside of his lip. I didn't know the appropriate conduct in a situation like this so I faked a smile for him. He still didn't see me. He sucked his teeth and threw a fist into the wall beside him. My smile crumbled and I suddenly wanted to disappear.

"What do I do? I saw everything! I know Sheldon wouldn't want me to say nothing to the police, but this is different, right?" I asked. I was not crying but randomly tears would roll down my cheeks. Damion looked at me sympathetically and said, "When school is over I'll call Tom. Me and him'll figure something out. I know you want to help, but you're definitely not ready."

Then he placed his hand on my shoulder. I couldn't believe him.

"What the hell are you saying?" I yelled. I sat up and shoved his hand off me. I've never yelled at him before. It all was spilling out of me. My face was heating up, contracting weird muscles. I tried to hold it together.

"Are you saying that because I'm a girl? Or because I'm younger? Because I'm just two years younger than you are! I can handle it just as good as you and Tom can. In fact, I'm handling this the best right now!" I started to cry. *Damn it*, I wanted to show him I could be calm. Once I started crying I couldn't stop.

"Look at yourself!" Damion shouted over me. "You can barely stand on your own. You're crying uncontrollably. You need to take it one step at a time!" He grabbed both my shoulders with his hands. I was swimming from the explosion of the moment. The tears were not only because of Sheldon, I thought, *I'm pissed off at you.*

"For God's sake, Blaise. You just watched your friend get murdered!"

I looked at him and let myself loosen up in his grip. As much as I hated to admit it, he was right.

"Fuck you."

He dropped his hands to his sides, keeping composure like he never heard me say it. He turned around and walked out of the room and closed the door. I sank into the bed and pulled the covers up to my chin. I cried softly for Sheldon, praying to God to help me wake up from this nightmare. I rolled to my side, facing the wall. I traced random and comforting words onto the wall with my finger until I fell asleep. *Bitch. Fuck. Shit. Damion. Blaise. Jesus? Dead. Sheldon. Fuck. Bitch.*

Something woke me up with a jolt. There was Tom, his fingers digging into my arms. He was shaking me and screaming some shit. "You little bitch! You didn't help him!" he screamed.

I looked at him half-asleep and realized I was no longer dreaming. Then I realized what Tom was saying.

"I-I-I..." Damion pulled Tom off me. Tom stumbled onto his feet and shook away from Damion.

"What's the matter with you?" Damion started, "It was that guy's gang!" He let go of Tom quickly. Tom glared at him, confused and psychotic looking.

"What guy?" They were face to face. Tom was a bit shorter than Damion. He was looking up at him, but he actually looked tough for the first time in his life.

"The guy Sheldon killed," Damion finished.

Tom didn't know about that. He was never supposed to, either.

"What?" Tom shrieked.

*Shit.*

Damion swallowed hard and bit his tongue, his face contorting again, the way it did when I first told him about Sheldon's death. He looked at me, his eyes pleading. I stared at my feet, realizing Tom would have had no second thought about kicking the shit out of me.

"Sheldon killed a guy, by accident. He just wanted to shake the guy up a bit, get some cash or whatever."

I finished, "Unfortunately, that guy was in a gang and they've been after Sheldon ever since. We were all sworn to secrecy. We couldn't tell nobody." I looked back at Damion, and he was looking at the ground as if knowing this would all turn out wrong one day.

"You're both liars," Tom declared.

I looked up at him in disbelief. Tom stared back at me with hate. "I can't believe you fell for this shit, Damion." Tom said disappointedly.

Then Tom walked out of the house slamming the doors. I looked back at Damion. His head was still down. We both stood there in silence. I was surprised that Tom would turn on me like this. I was his only friend. I introduced him to Sheldon. I thought he looked up to me, I thought he trusted me.

"Why would he think I betrayed Sheldon?" I asked.

Damion finally raised his head, his eyes wet. "Forget it!" he told me.

*We're a team now. I thought to myself. Tom betrayed us and now it's just Damion and me.* Hate was something that came very easily to me. Hate came easy to any teenager that noticed the world had imploded and you're the only one that saw it.

"Listen, Blaise. We both know Tom. He doesn't believe what really happened. He's angry. He might tell the pigs it was you or both of us that did this to Sheldon. So we better take off. Other people might suspect us, too. And you can't let the the Reds find out you were a witness."

I let out an almost hysterical laugh. "We can't run, and as if no one will believe us," I said, trying to reassure him how stupid he sounded.

He just looked at me and asked, "What did I just tell you? We know what Tom'll do."

I broke eye contact. If I didn't go with Damion I'd be alone. I needed him. I needed him to need me too. And Damion was probably right. Tom would most likely tell the police. I raised my head and Damion was watching me.

"I know you don't wanna get involved in this gang shit, but really, we might not have a choice."

All of a sudden Damion was different to me. He was no longer the older, charming, beautiful guy. He was just like me. He wanted me to be his new best friend. I imagined us drinking and flirting together, us pooling our weed together.

"Okay, Damion. I'll come with you."

He looked surprised, then satisfied. "Good, we'll go to your house and grab your clothes and things. Then we'll come back here."

I opened the door and walked out into the world, which suddenly felt colder.

When we reached my house I ran downstairs to my room, Damion behind me. I opened my closet, grabbed my bag and emptied out all my school stuff. I hadn't been bringing it to school lately so there were a bunch of unfinished assignments inside. Damion stared at the cover page I drew for my, 'My life as a movie' project. He threw it to the side. Maybe he noticed how hard I had worked on it because of all the eraser marks on it. Or maybe he thought I was talented.

Damion helped me throw clothes in my bag, sweaters, pants, shirts and whatever else would fit. I reached the top shelf to get my underwear, bras and socks. When everything was packed, Damion threw the bag over his shoulder. I felt a single butterfly flutter in my heart, like it surpassed the immaturity of the tummy and found something better. He was the only guy to ever rummage through my clothes without the intention of making fun of them, like Sheldon always did. "Where did you even find a yellow Garfield shirt?" I remembered Sheldon saying and laughing. I didn't want to admit that I stole it from my mom's ex because I thought it was cool.

"Do you have everything you need?" he asked.

"Yeah, I guess. Where will we go?" I asked.

"Don't you worry about it," he told me as he pushed me through the bedroom door. Why would a girl give up her own bedroom to run the streets with a boy that gave her a single butterfly?

"Okay, let's go back downtown and go to my father's place. We can meet up with Sheldon's gang at Randy's party. I know Tom won't find us there because he doesn't know where it is. Sheldon was supposed to bring him." Damion gave me a smoke.

"Everything will fall into place there," he finished.

I couldn't stop thinking about how messed my life was becoming. This was not supposed to be the theme for my, 'My life as a movie' project.

# CHAPTER 3

WHEN WE GOT BACK to Damion's apartment, we spent the rest of the night smoking joints, listening to music and imaging what life was going to be like on our own. I was looking forward to no more curfews or chores. I could get high whenever I wanted, even stay up all night and sleep all day.

It felt a little awkward being alone with Damion. This was the first un-chaperoned sleepover I'd ever had with a boy–and it wasn't even Sheldon. I knew Damion was trying really hard to act normal, too. When things got quiet we would both stare at the ground or fiddle with our hands and clothes. I realized all we ever had in common was Sheldon and smoking weed.

"Wanna know a secret?" I asked.

"Yeah," Damion replied raising one eyebrow.

"Tom's mom still beats him."

I don't know why we were being so cruel, but we both started to laugh. Tom had become our enemy.

"He used to tell people he got into fights and used the bruises as proof." We laughed so hard our eyes were tearing. The weed had really kicked in.

Damion told me how Amanda, a popular girl in my class, was no longer a virgin. That made me laugh even harder. My cheeks were starting to hurt. We did this all night. Shared secrets, gossip, smoked weed. It was so relaxing I was able to put the Sheldon incident out of my mind completely. I didn't want to think about it all. I didn't want the image of Sheldon lying bloody on the ground to creep into my vision. I just wanted to stay high, laugh and pretend everything was fine.

When it finally got really late and we were both starting to nod off, I went into the bathroom to change into a t-shirt and shorts for pajamas. I looked in the bathroom mirror. My t-shirt was all wrinkled and my eye's were bloodshot and squinty, but when I saw myself, I felt beautiful.

That was the first night I didn't need to cuddle in a nest of blankets. Sleeping beside Damion could be compared to the first few minutes of a sweatlodge. I felt safe and comfortable. I woke up the next morning remembering I wasn't in my own bed. At first I had a drowsy strange sense of, *where am I?* Then I opened my eyes and my mind caught up to reality. A deep, heavy pain centered in the middle of my chest. *Sheldon.* I pushed back the feeling and the thought of him. But my heart still ached. It was a homesick kind of feeling. I started to think about my mom. I allowed myself to daydream.

I remembered when my mom would get a big paycheck or win at the casino she would be happy all week. She'd take me out on shopping sprees and we'd spend the whole day together. If I was ever lonely or depressed she'd spend all night just watching movies with me in her bedroom. I never thought much before about our good times. It wasn't until I missed her that these thoughts came to mind. I wondered if she was feeling the same way–missing me and remembering all the good times we spent together.

Most of the time I felt like, to her, I was just the annoying, expensive consequence of loving my father. Sometimes I thought the only reason I was there was to be the presence that kept her from being alone. I felt sorry for my mom. She probably heard about Sheldon by now and may be thinking the worst of what happened to me. If she'd taken the time to notice my clothes were gone and my school work was sprawled on the floor, she could've put two and two together.

Last time I ran away from home was because she gave me an earlier curfew for skipping. She never looked for me. I knew because I stayed at Carly's house. That should've been the first place she looked, since we were best friends at the time. Carly was over almost every day and my mom hated her because we always got in trouble. She never liked many of my friends for that reason. It never occurred to her that I was the one who came up with all the brilliant 'get into trouble' ideas. Whatever Sheldon taught me I would pass on; it was definitely the kind of stuff to get you in trouble. All my friends thought I was cool for it. It was always like a competition for who could be the first to do something audacious, or who could do it better. My other friends felt I was so lucky to have someone like Sheldon in my life. He was the coolest.

I cuddled into the blanket, thinking about how different things were going to be. Me, Sheldon, Tom and Damion used to do all kinds of things together. We used to walk everywhere together; sometimes we'd walk for no real reason. Tom and I would dance together when Sheldon and Damion weren't around to call us lame. We'd put on his mom's old dance cd's and do goofy moves with each other. This is how I learned my jig. It had no real structure, I just moved my feet around real fast.

"Holy Speedy Gonzales! You can barely see your feet move!" Tom would joke.

I knew Tom's mom from hanging out at his house. She was really nice to me. She always said I looked hungry and fed me snacks that could amount to a whole meal. Most days, she looked like a pillowy comforter that you could dive into. Her skin was soft and she smelt like coffee and cupcakes. I had only ever seen her mad once. Tom and I were skipping school and eating our lunches early at the school park. She happened to drive by and recognize her son's big grey t-shirt. She came stomping up to us, red as a tomato and cursing, "I swear to God, Tom Dubois! You're not gonna be able to sit on a toilet after I'm done with you!"

I sat on the swing, my mouth wide open, forgetting all about the peanut butter and jelly bite still inside. She grabbed Tom off the swing by his hair then dug her long nails into his arm. Tom didn't flinch, didn't resist in any way. He just went easy and limp, like a submissive dog. She slapped him a couple times, whacking his head with her thick arms. She didn't seem to care that I was there watching. She acted like she didn't even notice me. After it was over, the three of us never spoke about it.

Sheldon was everything Tom wished he could be. Sheldon had no fear of adults, he had no fear of consequences. I remembered once how Damion wouldn't let me go biking around town with him and Sheldon because he thought I'd slow them down. I was hurt but tried to act like I didn't care or had lost interest in going with them anyway. Sheldon wasn't fazed that I was a girl and didn't think I would slow them down. He told Damion to shut up and then officially invited me to join them. I felt my heart skipping and I couldn't help but smile like an excited dork. I jumped on my bike and tried extra hard to keep ahead of them just to prove Damion wrong. This was how my first real crush happened. Sheldon had stood up for me, he made me feel special. My crush only lasted a couple weeks, but at the time, I thought for sure we were meant to be together.

Those guys had always called me a 'little girl,' because for a long time I was always trying to prove I wasn't. It was that particular day, on our bikes, that Damion really started to accept me as an equal friend. He started to accept me more and more as I kept proving I could do anything they could, and sometimes better. I knew that day my life was starting to change, and it scared me. I remember I wanted to talk to someone, and that someone was Sheldon. He understood me without thinking I was being lame.

Lying there beside Damion, my daydreams tapered off. My mind wandered back to Sheldon. For the first time, I cried because I hadn't tried to save Sheldon. If I had only called the cops first, or gone outside, or even called someone to help Sheldon. I should have known that he couldn't take on those three guys by himself. I wanted to wail, but I stifled my crying. I made sure that I didn't make any sounds that would wake up Damion. I wished I could have turned to

Damion and curled into him. I had never wanted a hug more than I did right then. *It's okay, Blaise. You're alright Blaise. Blaise, shhhoouushhh baby.* I soothed myself.

I got up and looked over at Damion. He had his back turned to me, still sleeping. I went to the bathroom to get dressed. My eyes were still kind of puffy, but less red than last night. When I went back to Damion's room he was up and dressed already. We were both quiet, making small talk. Neither of us mentioned Sheldon. It wasn't long before we headed downtown because Damion wanted to get some new clothes for the party at Randy's that night.

I had never really hung out downtown on a weekday before. There were business people in suits, acting like they didn't notice us kids or the beggars. Maybe they really didn't. Busy with their own important lives—we didn't exist to them.

I could relate more to the street people than to the business people. In the daytime, I thought it might be a fun life being a bum. They never had matching outfits or bothered to comb their hair. They could say weird things to us and we'd just laugh. Damion and I stopped at a corner when an old guy who was picking up cigarette butts looked at me. I smiled and offered him the last of my smoke. He graciously took it and said to me, "You know…I wish people still put pies out on their window sills."

Damion and I laughed.

"Me too, buddy." I said.

I had no money to shop with, but Damion did. He bought me a skirt. I was really excited about it. It was a denim skirt that made me look like a real teenager. I stood in front of the mirror in the store looking at myself. *I bet Sheldon would've thought I looked more like a teenager in this. He wouldn't be able to call me little girl in this.* My eyes welled up with tears. I shook my head; shook off that dark feeling and went to see what Damion was looking at. He had found himself some pants that were baggy all around. He had to wear his belt with them. We couldn't find anything else in that store, so we left.

"Do you like the skirt?" Damion asked as we walked.

"Yeah," I answered shyly. I felt embarrassed that he had to buy it for me. "Thanks." I said.

Damion put his arm around my shoulder. "No problem, Blaise."

In another store, I found a tight tube top that ended just below my bellybutton. I took a couple of shirts into the change room. I adored the tube top, but when I checked the price tag on my top it read thirty-six dollars! I sighed. I couldn't ask Damion for that. I tore the tag off and buried the shirt in the bottom of my purse.

"Nothing fit me," I said walking out of the change room. Damion was looking at his shirt in the mirror.

"I think I should buy this one, what do you think?" I checked out his shirt. It was like any other shirt but it gave him an extra bit of 'cool'.

"It's cool." I said, starting to feel my adrenaline rise. The shirt in the bottom of my purse was making my heart beat faster. Tom changed out of the shirt and went to the cashier. I went by the door to wait for him. I watched as they put the receipt in the bag and gave it to Damion. I tried to look casual, but I noticed my palms were beginning to sweat. We walked out of the store and I prayed the alarm wouldn't go off. It didn't. When we were a block away from the store, my heart rate returned to normal. I looked back to make sure no one had followed us. "Damion? You know that white tube top I was trying on?"

"Yeah, it was nice. Too bad it didn't fit," he said.

"Yeah, well it did fit, and that's why I got it!" I said as I opened the purse so he could peer in.

He smiled and put his arm back on my shoulder, "You rebel."

I was happy he didn't get mad at me. I had only ever stolen candy in front of him before. I was too excited to wait until we got back to Damion's place, so we stopped in a public washroom for me to change.

The streets were busy downtown. Cars sped by with music blaring or the drivers would be talking on their cells. Even though it was shady downtown during the day because of all the tall buildings, most people seemed to wear sunglasses. The wind was stronger between the buildings and I was worried my skirt would fly up to my chest, but luckily the denim was too heavy for that. I noticed for the first time grown men were turning their heads to look at me. Not for doing something weird or embarrassing, but because I finally looked pretty enough to deserve it.

It was seven o'clock by the time I had a shower, got dressed and dried my hair. While Damion was in the shower I put on my makeup. By eight o'clock I was ready to go. My makeup was done, my outfit complete, my hair styled straight and put into a ponytail. Damion was ready too; he looked handsome in a dangerous way, like he might shank you for looking at him funny. His eyes had a look of wisdom that most kids our age had not developed. His mouth was a thin straight line that still looked tender. I liked his face. He gave me a big puffy black jacket to wear. It had fur along the rim of the hood. It was new and looked really nice. We left his house and waited for our bus across the street.

When we got on the bus, I slid the black jacket under my butt, I did not want to be in direct contact with the public seat fabric. As I sat there staring out the window and I began feeling nervous about being at the party. *What if the guys who killed Sheldon had seen me in the window? What if they were going to be at the party? What if they were waiting for me, ready to kill the only witness?*

I didn't pay attention to where we were going, to the streets or anything on our way there, so when we got off the bus I was as good as lost. The house was across the street from a government housing complex that looked old and empty. I suppose the house was perfect for a party. It also looked old and run down. The eave troughs were barely hanging on, the paint looked dirty, white and chipped and the grass was overgrown to the point of being wild. It's not like the party could wreck the house any worse than it already was.

Even when we were standing outside the house I could hear the throb of the music from the party. I could feel the base pulsing in my stomach. It was cool but scary at the same time. Damion and I walked up the sidewalk stepping over broken glass on the ground. Three guys stood outside the house on the street. They were yelling and swearing at each other, but I couldn't make out what they were saying. They were all obviously drunk. One guy seemed more nervous than the others as he tried to mediate and calm the situation down. But the swearing escalated to pushing and then finally turned into a fight. Suddenly, a few people came running out of the house and circled the fight. I wanted to stop and watch too but Damion only slowed down for a moment, glanced over at them, and continued on to the house.

When we got closer to the front door I noticed one slutty-looking girl standing with two older guys. She had bleached blonde hair, gross makeup and was giggling and acting really drunk. They had their hands all over her and she seemed to be enjoying the attention. Damion looked at me, "Don't separate," he said, and looked at me with a serious look on his face. I looked back at him and nodded my head in agreement. Now I was worried about the shirt I was wearing. It resembled the outfit the girl outside was wearing. I didn't want to go inside, but I followed Damion closely, practically right on his arm. I was mostly nervous about standing out— not fitting in. These people were older and didn't care about anything but a good time. I wanted to be one of them but I wasn't yet. I felt younger. I wanted to know what it would be like having someone like Damion come up to me and tell me I'm the prettiest girl in the room.

It was crowed walking in the house. There were so many people at the party. I looked around the living room. I saw people drinking, but what really caught my eye were the people passing joints around. Although I smoked weed before, it was always while outside or hiding in bedrooms with my friends. One time my uncle caught me with drugs. He came to our house when my mom wasn't home. I tried to put everything away when he walked in my room but it was too late. I was busted and could tell from the anger in his eyes. In my mind I saw him as a cowboy. His boots were tapping on the ground in rhythm, and he was palming his keys like they were a whip. From then on I never wanted to be caught again, so I became a bit sneakier.

Once we were in the living room I noticed a door left slightly open and some people sitting near a partly open door, snickering. Inside that room it was dark, but I could see the end of a bed. I saw movement and immediately turned my gaze away, feeling like I was violating something meant to be private. I wondered if the couple on the bed were being liberated, oblivious, or purposely trying to shock people.

Damion steered me over to the couch where a group of people from Sheldon's gang were smoking up. I've known about these guys ever since Sheldon killed that guy. We sat down beside them. Normally, this would be weird to do in a house full of strangers, but the truth was that there was no room anywhere else, and Damion wanted to talk to Sheldon's gang. I sat near the end of the couch beside a guy who seemed to be about eighteen-years-old. At first, they looked at us with curiosity. The guy beside Damion pointed at him, "I seen you around before. You're one of Sheldon's friends, right?"

Damion knew who the guy was, but he looked at him hard pretending he was trying to remember his face, "Oh yeah…I think I met you once before."

The guy smiled. Then he looked at me. "I don't know you though," he said as he pointed his finger towards me. Nervously my eyes shifted from him and then to Damion.

"That's my friend, Blaise. She's cool. She was a friend of Sheldon's too."

The guy's name was Fred. He shot Damion a look. "What do you mean by 'was'? Do you guys carry beef with Sheldon or what?"

Damion looked at him in disbelief, "You don't know? You weren't told?" Damion shrugged his shoulders, "Sheldon's dead, man. He got killed by The Reds. Happened about two days ago."

Fred looked at us in horror. As Damion told the story, I sat there dazed and numb. I didn't want to listen to the details and relive it in my mind. But I also didn't want to be disrespectful, so I sat there staring at Fred's face. He had three big freckles on his nose that made up a lopsided triangle. It was the perfect number of freckles, one less and it would look like dirt, one more and it would be the only thing you could see. Damion told him about the bad situation we were in now. That we weren't sure what stories were going around about what happened. Or, if the Reds even knew anyone had witnessed the murder. He loosely suggested we should take Sheldon's place.

After Damion finished telling the story, Fred talked to us slowly and seriously, like a teacher does when they're about to say something that's going to be on a test. "Honest, I thought he just fucked off for a couple days, that maybe he'd show up tonight." He buried his head into his hands and then said, "Do you understand our rule about what happens when one of us dies?" He lifted his head to make eye contact with both of us.

"No." I answered. *Has anyone in this gang died before Sheldon?* I wondered.

"Well, you wanna take his place?"

Damion and me exchanged looks and Damion nodded his head, yes.

"Okay, but you have to get initiated first. That's the rule. Cool?" He asked.

"Is that seriously a rule?" I asked.

"Shut up, Blaise. Of course it is. I told you that." Damion looked annoyed with me. Like my stupid question was going to mess everything up. I didn't say anything else. I guess it was supposed to be a rhetorical question.

"Good, we'll initiate you later tonight...after the party," he said with a smile as he passed Damion a joint. I sat there confused; wasn't I in the plan too? I didn't want to be left out, no matter what.

"What about me? Can I be initiated too?" I asked.

Fred looked me up and down, "I guess there's no harm in that."

What Damion could do, I could do too. Maybe he didn't really invite me because he was waiting for me to ask. I hoped it wasn't because he thought I was just a skank that came along to the party with Damion. Either way, I took it as a challenge to my capability and I wanted to take him up on it. But what if I messed up and didn't do as well as Damion for some reason? Would they take him in and turn me out? *Damion wouldn't let us get separated like that...would he?*

When the joint got passed to me I took a hoot and kept it passing. When the weed kicked in I felt paranoid. I wanted to be in the corner somewhere with Damion so we could laugh at all the stupid shit we laughed about the night before. But I couldn't do that. These guys didn't seem the least bit high, even Damion. I felt like a I was the only one getting buzzed—and way too buzzed. I sank into the couch and wanted it to swallow me up. I hated being the highest one, and being paranoid was ruining my buzz.

People were coming and going. At first I was on the end of the couch but now I was more in the middle. A guy sat down beside me and tried to talk to me several times. I tried to keep it short, sinking myself deeper into the couch. Whenever I wasn't looking he'd rub my leg. At first I pretended not to notice, then he'd slide his hand higher. I slapped his hand fast and he recoiled with surprise. Then I got scared he was going to get pissed off. To my surprise he just kept talking. I sighed in relief and turned back to Damion's conversation with Fred. The guy beside me tried again. His hand started massaging my thigh as he spoke to me casually, slurring and trying to give me sexy eyes that, instead, looked like floating buttons. I nodded my head and said 'uh-huh, uh-huh,' even though I had no idea what he was saying. I nudged Damion. He swirled around and looked at me, "Yeah?"

I nodded my head towards the guy. He was still talking drunkenly, not catching on. Damion got up and shot a fist into the man's face. I held in my scream. I didn't think he'd handle it like that so fast. I just wanted him to tell him to fuck off or something. Then the guy stood up. Damion raised his head high while still looking down at him, "Don't touch her."

The guy smiled. "I'll touch whatever I want."

I could see the anger in Damion's face. He hit him again, and the guy flew backwards. The guys on the couch started laughing. "Go Damion! Show us what you got!"

The guy got up and wiped the blood off his nose. "You bitch!"

He threw a punch back at Damion but it wasn't quick, so Damion blocked it and threw another punch. The guy grew frustrated and pulled out a shank. Damion's eyes widened, but not for long. He looked at Fred, who smiled, grabbed an empty beer bottle from beside him, and threw it to Damion. Damion grabbed it and swung it at the guy's head. The guy went down but came up charging with the switch out again. Jumping out of the way, Damion hit the guy in the back of the head. He went down again, but this time he stayed down. I got worried; did Damion make the same mistake as Sheldon had?

This fight was like fights I'd seen before. Even kids at school would try swinging knives around. But I was still shaken up by what happened to Sheldon and I knew that it could actually happen again.

Fred said, "Ha! Ha! Knocked'im out good! You're a real fighter, Damion!"

We both sighed in relief.

"Hey, let's gank some of his stuff!" Fred continued.

I looked at Damion and he shrugged. I wanted to be accepted as much as Damion seemed to be, so I was the one who bent over him to search his pockets. I found three grams of weed and a wallet. I passed the marijuana to Fred and took the wallet. The rest of the gang dragged the unconscious guy out of the room and threw him outside. I proudly showed Damion: fifty bucks! It was the first time I was ever fought over. I never felt more like a woman in my life.

Early in the evening time flew by, but as the night wore on it slowed to a crawl. We couldn't stop talking about Damion's fight. Every minute felt like an hour. My new buddies told me that it was because of all the weed. I was wasted, and so was Damion.

Damion started to get rowdy and flirted with any girl that walked by. He was getting cocky from all the attention because of his fight. He started to leave me behind to bask in the light of his new popularity. Some guy came along and kept giving me drinks. We sat on the floor and talked. At first I thought he was a little weird but as time flew by my impression changed. He seemed to listen to everything I had to say. I spilled my guts about Sheldon and told him I was staying with Damion because I ran away from home. I talked about everything I could think of, like how Sheldon had been my best friend, how Sheldon was always the one to see me as more than just a girl. He always tried to treat me like one of the guys and trusted me with the secrets only best friends would know. I didn't tell him about the guy Sheldon had done in.

I told him about how Sheldon always listened to me. I began to tell him about the time that Sheldon stood up for me when some girls at school were making fun of me. I remembered the day that Sheldon skipped school and showed up at mine. I remember sitting alone because Carly was at a dentist appointment. I noticed everyone shift towards the entrance, whispering and gossiping. I turned to see Sheldon and smiled instantly. I jumped out of my seat and ran over to him, excited he had come to my school.

Sheldon almost ignored me, like he was pretending he didn't know me. He asked, "Where's those bitches you were telling me about, Blaise?" I inadvertently looked toward the group of gossipy girls that were always picking on me, but then I quickly turned back to Sheldon.

I got nervous that everyone might have heard him. I prayed that whatever he did, that it didn't make my situation worse. Everyone fell silent and just stared at Sheldon, anticipating would come next.

"You!" he walked passed me and pointed to the prettiest girl in the group, "You're the bitch that gave me chlamydia, you dirty bitch! No one touch her, she's got chlamydia! I'm sending you my doctor's bill you dirty slut!" He left the cafeteria, then he yelled from the hallway, "You best believe you'll be hearing from me again!"

The guy sat there listening to my stories, nodding his head with an understanding smile and kept refilling my drink as I drank. We were both drunk. Out of the corner of my eye I saw a man staring at me. I looked back at him every now and then, and he was still there. He was tall with a muscular build, green eyes, dark skin and dark hair. I liked him noticing me. The guy who'd been filling my drinks was starting to pass out. I stumbled over to Damion and kind of collapsed on the cushion beside him. He smiled and made room for me. I leaned on his shoulder and soon fell asleep.

I awoke with a jolt; Damion was screaming at me to wake up. When I painfully lifted my eyelids, he grabbed my hand and started running out of the house. Being jolted awake while I was drunk caused me to have a foggy understanding of the situation at first. I felt sick to my stomach. I stumbled along and Damion pulled me as he ran. Everyone was running out of the house. The farther we ran, the smaller our gang got. The group kept splitting in half into smaller groups. Some headed for the street while others took back alleys to jump fences, which me and Damion thought safest as well.

"Where are we going?" I asked, still half asleep and nauseated.

Fred and the rest of the gang started climbing a fence.

One gang member, the tallest one, yelled, "Hurry up you two, the pigs are coming!"

Damion helped me climb. I was so dizzy I could hardly see. The gang helped me on the other side. I was standing beside the tallest gang member and he asked me if I was okay. I nodded my head but I felt green in the face. In the distance I could hear the sirens. Damion and another boy were still on the front side of the fence. The sirens grew louder. Damion and the boy jumped the fence quickly and we all bolted down the alley. I ran in a blur through the dark, hauling myself over old ratty fences that could collapse under the weight of a single person, until we made it to the tall guy's house.

# CHAPTER 4

WHEN I WOKE UP I rubbed my face, all poked and bumpy from the carpet imprint. Carpet fuzz tickled my nose. I rolled over and saw Damion asleep on the ground two feet away from me on his back. I got up quietly because this was the first time I had ever woken up in a unfamiliar house. I felt nervous that someone's mom or dad might walk in, notice me and yell at me for trespassing.

A boy was lying on the couch, awake and watching tv. He had jet black greasy hair and his face had a greasy film covering it. I sat straight up but he didn't seem to notice. He said nothing to me, didn't acknowledge me at all. I reached over and poked Damion.

"Wake up," I whispered.

Damion rubbed his forehead and sat up. For a moment I thought we had slept at the party but then I realized it was a different house. It was in the same condition as the other one. The wall beside me had spilt juice stains running down it. I had a feeling that the paint was originally white, not the eggshell grey it was now. As my senses awoke, the smell of sweat and old beer farts kick-started my morning-after headache.

A girl with a completely obvious bleached-hair job walked in the room and came up behind me. I wasn't sure if she lived in the house or had just passed-out there like me.

"What's up with you? Hungover?" She asked in a friendly tone. I nodded yes.

"Don't worry. What works for me is a nice hot shower. Usually sleep and silence work best, but you won't find much of that here."

I thanked her for the advice and got up. She led me to the washroom and taught me how to lock the door using a kitchen knife.

"I'm Lindsay, by the way," she said.

"I'm Blaise." I said as I grabbed the knife and closed the door.

"Hope you feel better." She said as she walked back toward the living room.

The bathroom paint color was smoker's teeth yellow…but done on purpose. The floor reminded me of public showers. The towels hanging on the rack were all used. They had fingerprints and stunk like sour, wet laundry, so I decided I would have to do without. I washed up fast using what I could from the tiny pink bar of soap, pretending to myself that I never noticed the hair stuck to it. When the tap turned off, I stood in the tub dripping, feeling dirtier than when I woke up. I tried brushing off all the excess water and twisted and shook my hair to get it somewhat drier. I wanted to get out of there fast because all I could think of was how there were probably millions of invisible bugs crawling up my feet from the tub floor. I jumped out of the tub and wiped the fog off the mirror. I had streaks of black makeup running from my eyes. I used the sink to scrub my face harder until it was clean and makeup free.

My mouth tasted like crap, so I squeezed a little toothpaste on my finger and did my best to scrape the fur off my teeth. By the time I was done, my body had dried a little. I managed to put my clothes back on; it's not easy getting dressed when you're wet. My clothes stunk like smoke and beer and made me feel dirty again. The only thing that didn't stink like smoke was my hair. Before I could feel sorry for myself and miss home I thought, *at least I'm free.*

I walked into the living room, which had filled up with more people. There was a bluish haze of weed and cigarette smoke hovering in the air.

*Fuck. Now my hair was gonna smell the exact same as it did last night.*

I noticed Damion was talking and making friends without me. I felt a little jealous and went to sit by Lindsay instead.

"So," I said, "what're we doing?"

She looked at me. Her eyes were already red and squinted.

"Getting high." I nodded my head in agreement. I had never done a 'wake and bake' before.

I felt my stomach rumble, and being aware of Lindsay's stoned–munchies state I decided to take advantage.

"Are you hungry?" I asked.

"Yeah, actually."

"Is there anything we can eat here?" She seemed like she would know. After all she had shown me how to use the bathroom door knife-lock.

I followed her into the kitchen. She opened a cupboard that was full of empty plastic containers and reached in for a bag of chips. She opened it and started munching by herself.

*Please, please offer me some.*

I looked at her, trying to send a message with my thoughts that I was hungry, too.

She pointed at the opening of the bag. I smiled and dived in. The chips seemed horribly damp but I kept going, not sure if it was going to be the only thing I'd eat for awhile. Lindsay chewed with her mouth slightly open. I thought it looked kind of cute as opposed to disgusting. If I tried to do that I wouldn't be able to look as cute .

The only other girl in the house besides Lindsay and I was Sarah. Sarah never talked to me, but mostly just hung out with the guys. She was really butch and kind of chubby. She was a bit too weird looking to be considered unnoticeable. She dressed like a man and looked like a street kid. She wouldn't last a month in high school.

Everyone was relaxing in the living room. Damion was sitting with Fred. He told Fred, while looking over at me, that me and him needed to pick up our clothes and things. He also mentioned that he still had five grams of weed at his house.

"Yeah, they gotta go to Damion's house to pick up their stuff anyway. We might as well go with them and smoke that weed." Fred announced to the gang.

Since there was pot involved, the rest agreed. There were fifteen of us in total. Me, Lindsay, Sarah and twelve guys.

We all started out to Damion's. It was kind of chilly outside. I used one hand to pull my jacket closer together and the other to shield my eyes. The sun was extremely bright and made my headache worse. I kept my eyes on the pavement, trying to think of something other than my brain swelling and pulsating against my skull. I started scanning the sidewalks for wrappers. *–One–Two…*

It took us about twenty minutes to get there, but it felt like a lot longer. I think it was because Lindsay was being flirty with Damion the entire way and it was getting on my nerves.

"Blaise, use the hood on the jacket!" Damion said.

I kept scanning the ground while I flipped the hood as far towards my face as I could. I wanted him to ignore Lindsay and hold my hand or something. I didn't want to be his girlfriend or anything, I just wanted a sign that I wasn't being left out.

I started to ask Damion a question, "Hey, can we get something to eat at –"

Lindsay's laugh drowned me out and Damion turned away from me. I felt a hot rise of jealousy. I couldn't even finish one sentence without her interrupting, complaining about her thong or something else that was so stupid it made me feel physically sick just to listen to her.

When Damion unlocked the door to the apartment I rushed in and got my things. It took about five minutes to throw all my shit into the little school bag. Damion hurried too. I guess he didn't want to have fifteen kids mess up his dad's place. Or he was just uncomfortable being in a little place crowded with rowdy people. Damion grabbed his weed and went into the living room to join his friends. I threw the bag over my shoulder and followed behind him.

"We're all ready! Let's go!" Damion yelled to the gang.

I ran into the kitchen as the others started filing out. I grabbed some boxes of Kraft Dinner, a block of cheese, and some crackers, threw them in my bag and ran to join them. I felt like such a squatter having a stash of food in my bag. I wanted to bash Lindsay's head into the door, tell everyone it was nice to meet them but I had a really important family reunion I couldn't miss. I felt like just going home and facing the music.

We all piled out of the tiny apartment and talked about where we should go to smoke up. While walking, I occupied myself by digging in through my pockets to look for extra money or something. Sadly, I found nothing. I decided to move on to my purse, where I found my wallet and a hairbrush. I dug a little deeper until I found something unusual; it was a plastic bag. I pulled it into view and realized it was Sheldon's weed. Then I remembered I also had his switch. Damion was ahead of me. I sped up my pace to catch up with Damion.

"I just found Sheldon's weed in my purse! Should we smoke it?" I whispered.

"Yeah, I guess so, nothin better to do with it." I passed him the baggy but kept the switch for myself. It was the only thing I had of Sheldon's and it was sentimental to me now.

We walked a few blocks down the street from the apartment until we found a park. Lindsay was still working on Damion, even by the time we got to the play structure. There was a guy named Justice who was looking at me a lot and I knew he was talking about me. He would be talking to Fred while staring at me, and then Fred would look at me too. I never felt as awkward as I did then. Since Damion was busy being a piece of meat for Lindsay, I had no one to 'play it cool' with. I pretended I was involved in Damion and Lindsay's conversation and played with my hair, trying to look like I didn't notice Justice, even though it was increasingly obvious he wanted me to. I climbed onto the structure behind Damion, and Lindsay quickly sat between us. If it wasn't for her constantly smiling sweetly at me, I would have assumed she hated me.

The joints started going around and I let the weed fade me out. I should have been trying to bond with people but I just wasn't as interesting as Damion. My head started feeling heavy and my eyes kept thinking I was dreaming.

Justice was hot, though. He had perfect teeth, which were more noticeable when he was with Fred. He was really tall and looked much older than sixteen. Plus, if he thought I was worth staring at, when I wasn't even trying to get his attention–that just made him seem even hotter.

The park had monkey bars and a climbing gym that a bunch of us were sitting on. The rest were standing around as we passed joints back and forth. Damion reached over Lindsay to tap me on the leg.

"How's it going?" his eyes were totally red and his upper lip was stuck to his gums in a dried up smile. This reminded me of my own dehydration.

"Thirsty."

Lindsay convinced Damion to play tag with her, always letting herself be caught. Instead of actually tagging each other they would tackle or hug. It was a completely obvious slutty thing for her to do, but truthfully, I really wanted to trade places with her.

I knew that Damion and I were supposed to get initiated that night. I was kind of hoping it would be a dare or a scavenger hunt but I knew things didn't really happen that way. I was kind of looking forward to being a troubled teenager. I always admired the kids that were really messed up, it made them more interesting than those of us who weren't. All anyone in this gang was really able to brag about was beating people up. Justice was talking about how he once beat up a street watch guy because he was trying to tell him to go home.

"It was almost like beating up a cop," he said.

I smiled back at him. He reminded me of Brad Pitt in the movie Fight Club. And anyone who could remind me of Brad Pitt was worth a smile.

"Are you guys going to fight those girls?" I asked, as I stuck out my lips in their direction. Most of the people that walked by us tried to act invisible, but these girls were coming right up to us. I thought they'd laugh or something but they didn't. We all became serious and stared at the girls. I noticed Lindsay and Sarah pull out a shank and a set of brass knuckles. Fred approached me, "That's K.O.B. They'll probably try to fight the girls first, so I want you to use this."

My stomach knotted. He handed me a billiard eight-ball. I muttered, "Thanks." *They couldn't possibly expect me to use it?*

I put the weapon in my jacket pocket, but kept it wrapped around my hand. K.O.B. stood for Killing Off Bitches. It was a girl gang known for being really dirty fighters, or so I heard from Lindsay. One of the girls walked up to Lindsay, Sarah and me.

"What gang you guys from?" She was tall and blonde.

"W.B., West Bloods." Sarah said, not smiling.

"Let's go then."

Sarah pulled out her eight-ball, but then punched the girl really hard in the face. The girl almost crashed to the street but managed only to stumble backward. Sarah pushed her, then started wailing the eight-ball on her. I assumed that these weapons were more for defense and intimidation, but Sarah obviously didn't think so. When the girl fell to the ground the fight broke out. I got scared at first, especially when one of them came charging at me with a knife. I whipped the eight-ball out of my pocket and swung it towards her. It must have hit her because she didn't get me. She went a bit farther than me. I took advantage of this by crashing the ball into the small of her back. Then I shot her another one to the arch of her back. She fell to the street and rolled onto her back as though to protect it. I smashed the weapon into her ribs and then again in the chest bone. I looked around and everyone was in a scrap. My adrenaline was pumping and I felt scared about what just happened, but I didn't want anyone else to see that.

All of a sudden a piercing pain went through my side. I screamed and flung the eight ball around with me. I hit the girl right in the nose! She went down with a single blow. I held in the scream and was mortified. The fight was still on, but all I could think of was my beginner's luck had worn off. I touched my side where I got hurt and noticed a bit of blood. It started hurting intensely after I saw the blood.

*Fuck. Shit. This is gonna make me so cool. Bitch, that hurts!*

Paul exclaimed, "Hey I seen that! That was so cool the way you knocked her out!"

"I know."

I nodded my head and held my side, which kept bleeding.

"Hey Blaise, you're bleeding!" Justice exclaimed, as he pointed to my side.

I looked at him in disgust. "Well, duh!" I yelled. "Get me something to stop it!"

They all looked at me like I might be on my deathbed or something. It was more like a deep scratch than an actual cut.

Fred and Justice looked around for something to help me. I felt bad about yelling at them, I really didn't want them to think I was a bitch. Fred's little brother, Sam, gave me his shirt to use as a bandage. I knew I didn't need it, but I think everyone was enjoying the drama of me being seriously injured. I took the shirt and thanked him. He helped me wrap the fabric around my body and tie it up tightly.

By the time we finished with my wound the fight was over. Sarah was the only other one to get hurt, and she just got hit in the head. Everyone crowded around me, asking if I was all right over and over. Damion pushed to the front to see me.

"Let's go back to the house!" Damion said to everyone. "I need to bandage Blaise properly! She may have to go to the hospital!" Everyone nodded and started walking in silence. I wanted to laugh, but I wanted to hug Damion even more. Fred walked up to me and shook my hand. "You know how to use that eight-ball pretty fuckin good."

I looked down, hiding my own pride, liking his praise. I felt happy that Fred accepted me. I was fitting in easier than I thought. As we started walking back to the gang house Damion pulled me over to him. "I'm still your best friend.

You can trust me with anything, and you know that, right?"
He kissed me on the cheek. I nodded my head once again. I
pulled out a cigarette and lit it. It calmed my nerves slightly.
It sounded like he was talking more to himself than to me.

Back at the house we finished off the rest of the weed. It
made me feel like it was all just a dream. My thoughts were
starting to get all screwed up, nothing made sense, but I felt
like the smartest person in the gang. I let Damion bandage
up my side in the bathroom. It stung when he poured water
on it. I bit into my bottom lip, but I didn't whine. I'm sure
he noticed how much of an 'un-emergency' my cut really was
now, but he didn't say anything about that. I'm also pretty
sure by the way he was being around me that he noticed I
was acting different, too. Shit, I used to cry when kids would
tease me at school, let alone getting cut.

*Get a grip, Blaise. It's cool. It barely even hurts.*

Damion raised an eyebrow when he saw me chewing my
bottom lip and staring at the ceiling.

"We're alone now. You can cry now you big baby!" he
teased.

I glared at him.

"Who's crying? I'm just hungry!"

He rolled his eyes and left me in the bathroom. I lifted
my shirt to my belly to see my bandage.

*Hardcore. Sheldon would've never thought I had it in me to be
in a fight like this.*

•••

Justice became really loud when he got high. When
we got back home and had smoked a few, Justice had no
problem flirting. He was all over me, whispering things in
my ear. I wanted to smack him a good one. He said things
like, "You won't regret it. I can make you scream." Then I felt
his wet tongue on my neck. I put my hand on his shoulder
and pushed him off me. Getting up off the couch, I walked
over to Damion. He and Lindsay, Fred and Jack, were sitting
on the floor by the window, rolling joints and cigarettes. I

knelt down beside him and watched everyone, wondering what I could do to seem more like them.

I smoked more pot that day than usual. I couldn't stop. No one else was stopping, and I felt like I was sticking out enough as it was. I started feeling paranoid. I let my mind wander and daydream about those girls from the K.O.B. They must've been really pissed by that time. I tried to imagine what would happen if I went back to school and they found me. It would either be incredibly cool or embarrassing, especially if I got my ass kicked.

Justice stood up, "Yo! Listen up!" Everyone turned to face him.

"When is Blaise going to get initiated? I think we should discuss that now."

Fred smiled at him and then at me.

"I guess now would be a good time!" Fred replied.

I sat upright. Everyone was looking at me. I hated being the center of attention. It felt even worse because I had smoked so much weed and was suffering from paranoia already.

"Wait a minute!" Lindsay started, "She was in a fight, and with two people. That should count as her initiation."

I looked over at Lindsay and smiled at her thankfully. She returned the friendly smile. Fred sat there for a minute, thinking. "I guess she has a point there. You're in." Fred smiled. It was as simple as that.

I was relieved that conversation was over. A sense of pride washed over me for getting into the gang. Wow, I was in. Like, I just got to live every little girl's dream. Everyone was still looking at me but I didn't care anymore.

I sat beside Damion on the floor by the window. He nudged me and smiled. I wanted him to be Tom's mom for a moment. I wanted to fall into a place where only the smell of cupcakes and coffee could've taken me.

Lindsay leaned over and said to me, "I knew you'd make it! We're gonna have so much fun together girl!"

"Let's party!" Sam, Fred's little brother, screamed over our conversation. He had just come through the door with a 24 case of cheap beer cans. Everyone passed them.

Damion started chugging his beer right away. He looked at me from the corner of his eye and wrapped his arm around me. I closed my eyes and pretended for as long as I could that he was Sheldon.

# CHAPTER 5

I WAITED IN THE KITCHEN while Andy cooked up a few packs of Kraft Dinner. By now, I knew I'd have to grab dishes fast if I wanted to eat. I talked with him, holding a plate and fork in my hand and I convinced him to let me fill my plate after him. Others began pouring in, diving for plates or bowls. It would probably be easier just to steal or get money and go out to find food, but when you're lazy and it's lunchtime, plate diving was more convenient.

In my first week at the house, I was taught how to get money. We were divided into groups of three and told to go our separate ways and jack people. I was first sent with Lindsay and Sam. Damion went with Justice and Fred. They always had the most success. I had a hard time stealing from other kids around my age. Money at that age is hard to come by and they probably worked hard for it. I had some guilt over it, but no one was more important than me and my friends, so I did what I had to do. Lindsay was good at picking the right kids to jack. Sam looked threatening enough that we hardly ever had to use force. Of the people we jacked, maybe one out of five would force us to act on our threats.

One girl just didn't want to give up her money so I punched her in the nose while Sam held her back. Later I had a confused sense of guilt and pride. But when we added up the money, which came to one-hundred-and-twenty dollars, the pride eventually outweighed the guilt and I began to feel like I really fit this life.

The best place to rob people turned out to be in the nicer part of the city. It made sense: fewer cops, more kids with more money, and the people in the area weren't expecting it. If we stayed in the slums past downtown and more into the north end, we'd get more trouble and less money. I always felt more nervous there because we were closer to my old neighbourhood. I didn't want to run into my mom, or anyone else I knew. But as time went on and I got more used to it, it got easier.

Sometimes before a party we would steal new outfits from stores. Some people in our gang didn't steal, so they always had to wear their old outfits. Stealing from a store never scared me, and I never felt bad. I justified it, thinking if the store owners could afford to wear nice suits every day then they could spare a few cotton shirts for me.

Me, Lindsay, Sarah, Damion and a few others usually went out shoplifting. Of course, we had to separate so that the clerks wouldn't be able to keep an eye on all of us at once. Before the first time I went with Lindsay and Sarah, Sarah rarely used to talk to me. As we walked to the store together, it was the first time I had a chance to really look at her. She rarely washed her face, which I knew from living with her, but now I could see it on her. She looked like she had wet dust hiding in every fold in her body. She would either wear day-old makeup or just paint over it with new make up. Her teeth were unusually small, which was not very noticeable because she rarely smiled and she always smelt like greasy hair and rained-on clothes.

Neither of the girls thought I stole things, and when I did they treated me a lot better. On that first time, I walked out of the store with a Popsicle, candy and two magazines. After that, Sarah started talking to me. Before, she'd just acknowledge me, then talk to Lindsay.

Lindsay and I planned to go shoplifting for new clothes one day, so she got Fred's backpack. I offered Damion a chance to join us but he told me that he didn't need any more clothes.

"You just make sure that you don't get caught," he told me as we walked out the door.

I answered him with a cocky smile, "I never get caught."

It was early evening so the stores would only be open for about another hour by the time we got there. As we began to walk, a light rain came down, but Lindsay and I didn't care. The street lights were already on and the road looked wet and smooth. I always thought my hair looked sexy when it got wet. Sheldon thought so too. I looked up at the sky as the rain washed down my face. I missed Sheldon. The hem of my pants started to get soaked. I used to make fun of Tom for having pants that looked like this. It made me laugh a little inside.

"So, you and Sheldon were close, hey?" Lindsay started talking as we walked to the bus stop, only a block away.

"I remember when we used to have sex, he was good. Did you and Sheldon ever get that close?"

I looked at her, surprised. No one had mentioned him since I had moved to the house, and I guess I wasn't expecting it.

"No, we were just friends, the whole way through," I smiled. "We knew each other since we were pretty young. Our moms would babysit for each other. As we got older, I remember he used to call me 'little girl.' I don't think we ever thought of each other like *that*."

I didn't like Lindsay talking to me about Sheldon. It felt like she was violating me by asking about him. Talking about Sheldon was for just me and Damion. We were tight, me, Sheldon, Damion and Tom—although Tom was long out of the picture.

Lindsay smiled at me sympathetically, "You know, I actually heard of you before you came here. He talked about you a lot. You know that, don't you?" I was about to answer but she didn't let me.

"I think that's why you weren't questioned too much—we've all heard of you. He loved you from the sounds of it. You guys must have been really close. I guess that's why I asked."

I smiled, but it was hard. I felt like she just punched me in the stomach but I couldn't get her back. How could she tell me that Sheldon had feelings for me now that he was dead? How could I not have known it was what I wanted to hear for years?

One time I was upset because my mom ditched me for her boyfriend after she promised to spend the day with me. Sheldon met me down the street to hug me and let me cry. Whenever I had a problem he was there, no matter how stupid my reason to cry was. He'd walk me home and every time I'd shut the door behind him, I'd be smiling again. I wished he was still here. I wanted to meet him halfway down some random street between our houses and just cry.

We got off the bus in the most colourful neighbourhood in town. Osbourne. Colourful stores, graffiti, and interesting people. A lot of the city's homeless gathered in this area too, because somehow they fit in. There may have been color on the street, but there was also trash. It also looked like a place that Bugs Bunny would live, if he were real. I liked that street. The regular bums were there along with new ones. The one me and Damion had danced with way back when we first left home came up to me asking for money. It took a moment for him to recognize me.

"Ahh. You!" he smiled.

He pulled up his jacket sleeves and started his weak, sloppy dancing. As rough as my life felt at that time he made me realize it could be so much worse. His hair was disgusting and matted. Dirt permeated inside the creases of his deepest wrinkles. Lindsay laughed kind of confused like, but not in a malicious way. He kept dancing for her and she loved it like I had, but that day it just made me want to cry. I pulled Lindsay away to get to the stores in time.

"We gotta go," I told her, and loud enough so he could hear too.

"HEY! Got change!?" he yelled as I dragged Lindsay away by the arm.

"No, I don't." Lindsay yelled back.

He threw his hands up and kept walking in the other

direction. I brought her to the store Damion first brought me to after we spent the night at his dad's. That was only a few weeks or a month ago now, but it felt like it was a year ago. Lindsay brought me to the miniskirt section. She grabbed the shortest and sexiest ones.

I left her to look around for something else, but couldn't find anything. Then, I heard Lindsay call, "Hey Blaise, come here! It's perfect!" She held up the skirt to show me.

"Blaise, this skirt is perfect for you! Try it on."

I took the skirt from her and checked it out. It was black, shiny patent leather, which made it look cheap and hookerish.

"Maybe this is more you. I couldn't pull this off." I handed it back to her.

I grabbed a white lacy tank top for myself and shoved it in my purse while Lindsay distracted the clerk asking about the price of a skirt. I left the store before her and had a smoke outside while I waited for her to come out.

We walked a block or so away before we sat down on a bench to look at our goods. The rain had stopped but the bench seat was still a little damp. Lindsay had gotten the tight black miniskirt that came up to just below her ass and a matching tight black tube top, which was also very small.

We were still a few blocks away from the bus stop so I lit another smoke. I only had seven left. I wanted to get up and keep walking because of the wet bench, but Lindsay gestured for me to sit back down.

"Justice will buy you more," Lindsay said. I nodded my head and took a drag of my cigarette. "If I tell you something, will you promise not to tell another single soul?" Lindsay suddenly asked.

"Yeah sure, of course you can."

"Okay, well. Everyone thinks I'm fourteen but I'm really twelve. Thirteen in a couple months." She looked at me, then continued, "Please don't say anything. Not even Sarah knows! I just trust you more than anyone. Everyone treats me like I'm just a slut–free sex. You see me as a person, not just a slut."

She stopped for a while. I felt bad about calling her a slut all those times in my head. She continued, "You're like the friend I never had, and I want you to know that whatever happens in this gang, I'll be right in there with you," she finished.

I looked at her with a smile. I was in shock. She was twelve, and she'd been having sex for over a year already.

"Twelve?" I repeated.

She nodded.

She bowed her head. I put my hand on her shoulder.

"Thanks for trusting me," I said, and she looked up and smiled sweetly.

She looked like she could have been older than me. I didn't know why this was such a secret now. Would they really do anything if she just confessed? Was that what she expected me to do for her?

As we sat there, the sky turned shades of dusk. Telling that one secret was like opening a flood gate. The next thing I knew, Lindsay started telling me all about herself. She opened up to the most serious conversation we'd ever had. She was involved in this gang for the last two years, which meant that she had been with them since she was only ten-years-old. I found out that she was native, too, like me. You couldn't really tell at first, but after she mentioned it and I looked closely, then I could see it in her. I asked her about her mother.

"My mother committed suicide a long time ago, when I was about six. My dad beat her and she was addicted to heroin. I guess she couldn't take it any more. It took the police about a week to find the body. They found her in the forest, down by St. Boniface. Some kid found her, actually." She started crying.

I knew she would have let me hug her, but it seemed too odd still. I felt I needed to be cautious, but we were also bonding. I was still reacting to the secret sharing part. Now that we were friends, and now that she was crying in front of me and opening up to me, it felt like we'd probably become best friends.

"I think Damion likes you." I told her, trying to cheer her up.

"Really?" she sniffed.

"Yeah, kinda."

She smiled to herself.

"I think Justice is kinda hot, too." I added. She laughed.

"He thinks you are, too. Hey!... wouldn't that be cool if me and Damion started going out and you and Justice did?"

*NO!* I thought, but instead just smiled again.

"Yeah, it'd be okay."

I imagined going out with Justice. He was at least two years older than me and that alone made me tingle thinking about him. If we went out he would be my first real boyfriend. He was the same age as Sheldon and Damion, same gang as them, same friends...they were all quite alike.

It bothered me to think about Lindsay and Damion together. I guess I felt territorial over Damion.

*Nothing to worry about. Spark a joint. Light a smoke. And, be friends.*

"Wanna get high?" I asked, changing the subject again.

"Totally."

No one was around, so we lit up a joint right there on the bench. I blew out the smoke and watched it float away until it dissolved into nothing. I missed Sheldon. Lindsay and I must have looked so stupid with our jeans all wet from dragging in the puddles and sitting on the bench. That's the kind of thing Sheldon would've noticed.

Lindsay was leaning against the bench, thinking about something. I stared at the grass and let my brain start feeling heavy; it started to weigh a lot. I imagined what life would be like as an ant. Each blade of grass like a huge tree. I wondered if I'd be a renegade ant that left the colony to enjoy a life of freedom, or if I'd just be a regular ant and do what all the others do.

"What about your family?" Lindsay asked.

"My mom sits around the house and has boyfriends over all the time. We don't talk much. How things work is, if someone's over, I stay out of sight and earshot because she'd just make me leave anyway. My father hasn't seen me since I was ten. He just stopped coming by, stopped calling. Haven't talk to him ever since then."

I felt tears well up at the mention of my father. That made me mad at myself.

"My mom and I never talk about him anymore. It pissed her off or made her upset to hear about him. He left her when I was eight or so for another woman. I met her once, but my mother never did. My mom asked me when I got home one time about what she looked like, and when I described her as young and skinny...she cried. I regret saying that now–I can understand how that would have hurt. She never mentioned him much again, unless it was to talk about what an ass he was."

"Wow... rough," Lindsay sighed.

"Not really."

We sat silently for a moment.

"I hate being in this gang!" Lindsay confided, "They're dumb. I wish they would all die so we could leave," she added quietly.

I was surprised. I had no idea this was what she'd been thinking. She always seemed like everything was fine. I thought she was okay with everything.

"Why don't *you* just leave if you hate it?" I asked.

"Are you kidding? They won't let me leave. They say it would jeopardize them. They say it wouldn't happen because I might tell the things that happen in the gang. Didn't you know that?"

I hadn't really thought about that either. I assumed that Lindsay must have already asked them about leaving if she knew that.

"Besides, where would I go?" She added, and she did have a point.

We finished our joint and headed toward the bus stop in silence.

We walked into the smoky house and put our bags down by the bedroom door.

"Hey, you guys smoking' up?" Lindsay yelled.

Laughter was all she had for response. She grabbed my

hand and dragged me into the living room. "Let's get really high before the party tonight."

I nodded my head even though I was still baked.

"Hey, Blaise," Justice said.

I immediately felt my face flush because I had a feeling someone must've told him I liked him.

"Hey."

"You look really hot tonight."

"Thanks." My hair and clothes were soaked and I knew this was a planned gesture and not a real compliment.

"Wanna hang out after the party?" he asked.

"Yeah."

He smiled, then I turned to Lindsay, who was smiling from ear to ear.

I sat down with Damion and nudged him, "Hey, blasted?" I asked.

He smiled and passed me a joint and answered, "Almost."

I watched Lindsay move from one guy to the next. If someone pushed her hand away, she'd look a little desperate, but she'd move on. Damion started giggling and teasing Lindsay. She loved it.

Damion was doing a lot more drugs then he usually lets himself. Maybe he was just trying to fit in. We hadn't been talking much lately, mostly just when he was high or wanted something like advice about girls. I felt like I was loosing my closeness with him and it made me feel slightly panicked. Other than Lindsay, Damion was all I had. It made me feel safe knowing he was there at night.

The time came to get ready for that night's party. We girls got the bathroom first and another small group of guys piled into the other room. I grabbed my new clothes and Lindsay stuck her switch though the doorframe to lock it. Sarah was already starting to take off her clothes. Modestly, I turned around to take mine off, quickly putting on new ones. I hate changing with other girls; I can't help but think they're looking at me.

By the time we were all ready, so was the rest of the gang. I put my hair up in a half ponytail, which, surprisingly, made me look older. My black pants and white tank top went well with the jacket I was borrowing from Damion. We were all made to wear black bandannas. Black was the gang color. Almost everyone wore them as a head bandana, but I wore mine like a bracelet, and no one seemed to care. I walked to the doorway and put my shoes on, and so did Damion.

He smiled at me and whispered, "You like Justice?"

I smiled back weakly. Did he somehow know about my conversation with Lindsay? "Yeah, I guess so." I wanted him to get jealous. I wanted him to be as scared of losing me as I was of losing him. I did up my jacket.

"Ready to go?"

I looked down at my shoes as I grabbed my purse, remembering how I wanted these black sneakers with white laces so badly for my birthday. I remembered waking up that morning and my mom not being there. She was still out from the night before. When she got home that evening she was holding these shoes, holding them out to me with a, "Happy Birthday, sweetie," look on her face.

I really wanted to miss my mom right then. I wanted to be alone so I could concentrate on how much I missed smelling her. Cigarettes and French Vanilla. Her raspy voice that can send shivers down your body, the voice that all her boyfriends can't stop talking about. *It's okay, Blaise. You're alright. It's gonna be okay. Shhhhhoousshh.*

Lindsay tugged on my sleeve and said, "I'm pumped to get wasted with you tonight, Blaise!"

Then I realized one of my laces was about to unravel.

# CHAPTER 6

THERE WERE A LOT OF people in the somewhat small house. Everyone, like us, had their own cliques. For the most part everyone stayed within them too. Some girls were dressed in a way that made them look cheap but still acted as though they were above everyone else at the party. They smelled of sweat and baby powder and treated their bad hair-doos like they were long, luscious locks.

At first I tried to stay near Damion, who seemed to have totally forgotten about me. As our gang entered the room I glanced around and noticed that people turned to look at us in our colors. The presence of our gang colours created a feeling of tension that surrounded us as we worked our way through the house. I kept a calm look on my face. I didn't want to look worried and make the gang appear vulnerable. I noticed a few people who looked familiar, like the boy who kept giving me drinks at that first party I went to with Damion about a month ago.

The living room was the size of an average bedroom. The party was crowded already. People seemed to hug all the walls, so there was a tiny circle of space in the center of the room. This party was like most parties I'd been to lately. They could be categorized into two different scenarios. They were either the perfect place to take acid (get tripping high) or they were a pervert's paradise–with many opportunities to take advantage of wasted girls. It wasn't a 'this or that' call, both scenarios applied. It was just about how you decided you would feel about it that day.

After a while I stopped following Damion around. He was beginning to find my company annoying. Lindsay said it was because I was 'cock-block.' Other girls might see me as a threat, or think I was his girlfriend. I ventured off on my own, ditching most of the gang who had made their way to the basement of the house where they had set up an invisible territorial zone. As I walked around alone, I felt like everyone was looking at me. I was smiling, open for conversation. The drink-boy from the other party waved me over to him. I had seen him earlier but finally acknowledged him, pretending I had just found him. He was wearing a Nike shirt and baggy black sweatpants and sitting on the floor beside the dining table full of red cups and empty bottles. His entire outfit was just two different shades of black. He reminded me of the boys in my high school who would hide their skinny bodies in big clothes. Something about that association made me feel friendlier towards him.

"Hey, how have you been?" He asked, casually.

"I've been fine."

"May I ask for your name again? I forgot."

"I'm surprised you even remember me," I started, "seeing how drunk you were that night. My name's Blaise." He introduced himself as Jon. We both giggled a little.

While I talked with Jon, I had a strange sensation of someone staring at me. I had that feeling of someone's eyes on me for what felt like a long time, driving me slowly to paranoia. Subtly, I scanned the room, trying to figure out who the creep was. The music was loud and there were a lot of people there, smoking, drinking and laughing. But when my eyes met a certain guy, I instinctively knew he had been the one staring at me. He was not the creep I assumed he was, but a guy I had met at another party a while back. Jon kept on talking to me but I was no longer listening to what he was saying. This other guy now had my attention. He looked about nineteen. Tall, slender, dark hair gelled and spiked. He had nice, naturally tan skin. I noticed he didn't dress the way all the other guys did. He dressed neatly, wearing clothing that fit him.

I was tempted to talk to this guy. Our one-on-one eye contact felt like we were reading each other's minds. I was interested in him and he was interested in me. Not wanting to appear over anxious, I got up off the floor to look for the gang. I found them still downstairs in the basement. The night was just beginning. Damion was already so drunk he was disgusting to look at. Lindsay was surprisingly sober.

"Hey, Blaise." Justice said as his eyes went up and down my body.

I immediately felt my face flush because I suspected someone must've told him I liked him.

"Hey." I replied

"You look really hot tonight." he smiled.

"Thanks." I said with a coy smile.

"Wanna hang out after the party?"

"Yeah, sure." I did like Justice, and even though I was thinking of the other guy, it's always good to keep all the options open.

He smiled then turned to wander around. Lindsay smiled from ear to ear.

She pulled me over and asked me where I was. I was glad that she cared. I didn't realize until then that I hadn't been asked a question like that in a while. I ended up telling her about the guy who was staring at me, and mentioned that I was staring back. He made me feel like the prettiest girl in the room.

She grabbed my shoulder. "You should go talk to him! Exchange numbers!"

I no longer had a phone number, but the gang's house did. I asked Lindsay if I could give out the house number.

"Don't worry!" She said, taking my hand and giving me the, 'oh-please' face.

She reached for a pen in her bag wrote the number on my palm. I smiled a thank you and turned away, when she grabbed me back.

"Aren't you gonna show me this handsome man?" She asked playfully.

"Yeah, sure. I guess so." I replied.

I really didn't want her to come, because I didn't want him to know I was in a gang. I was planning on telling him the bandanna was just a part of my outfit. Also, there was the problem of having her gawk at him before me even having a chance to introduce myself or my slutty friend.

When we got back upstairs, I introduced Lindsay to Jon instead. They ended up getting friendlier than expected. Eventually I was completely out of the conversation, and I decided that I looked like the clingy third-wheel. I went to the bathroom and stood in a fifteen minute line before getting in. I used the toilet, checked myself in the mirror and left. As I exited, the girl next in line furrowed her brows at me and gave me a, 'I'm-so-much-cooler-than-you' stare before she and her two friends piled into the tiny room and locked the door.

I returned to the dining room corner where Jon had been hanging out. "Where'd Lindsay go?" I asked.

"She left somewhere, probably went back to where you found her." I had kind of hoped she'd be talking with Jon, giving me a chance to make eye contact with that guy again, while still hanging out with a friend.

Jon offered me a drink. I smiled weakly and accepted it. I leaned back against the wall, wanting to take off the heavy jacket, but afraid of having it stolen. I swallowed the drink quickly. The alcohol burned my throat a bit. It was strong, but I didn't want to show that I almost couldn't handle it.

"Light a joint, buddy." I told Jon. He reached into his sweater pouch and pulled out a skinny, almost pathetic joint. But who's complaining? Smoking while drinking always created a surprise buzz for me, depending which one I did more of. We shared the joint and then a cigarette. I felt like exploring new highs. I had the urge to try a new drug that would make me excited and have something worth bragging about.

While Jon and I smoke and drank we talked and laughed at anything. Then out of the blue, the guy I wanted to meet was standing across from us talking with a friend. He looked right at me and my huge grin. I decided I was going to talk to him, but when I tried to get up to talk to him my bones felt heavy and weighed me back down. I knew I was buzzed, but this felt different. I had to fight to keep my eyelids open. I really wanted to talk to this guy before he left, but my head started to spin. All I remember thinking was *"How much did I drink? It couldn't have been that much."* I felt panicked; I had never lost control over my body before. I crouched forward and put my hands behind my back against the wall to push myself up. I failed, and almost fell on my face. Luckily, Jon was quick to catch me. He pulled me up into his arms. My legs were too weak to stand on.

"What the hell did we smoke, man?" I felt my voice come out low and blurry. If you could see words they would have splashed on the floor like vomit. Jon smiled as I began to pass out. I tired to fight the sensation of passing out, but resisting just put me into a spiral of tunnel vision. *Don't let this happen to me. Please God, if you exist... I promise...if you just...*

The next thing I knew I was lying down on a bed. I couldn't move my body. I was conscious but had to fight to open my eyes. When my eyelids finally opened, my vision was blurred at first. I slowly looked around the room. I could see a blinking number on the alarm clock, and then I made out a lamp. I was in an unfamiliar bedroom. I was lying on a heap of bedding in the middle of the mattress, like a sprawled out starfish. My body was so weak I felt like a marionette with all my strings tangled and if I tried to stand up I would fold up into a ball of flimsy elbows and bent knees. I didn't remember anything about how I got in this room. My eyes widened and narrowed as I tried to gain more focus around me.

I held in my breath as the realization of what happened came to light. I was the girl in the 'date rape' public service announcements, crumpled on the bathroom floor like dirty Kleenex. *Jon must've brought me here, how could that have happened?* As my brain spun out of its throbbing dizziness, I wished this was just a bad dream, but knew it couldn't be. I wished I could wake up and realize this day never happened. All my worst dreams are ones where I can't wake up. I closed my eyes again for a moment, in silence, and talked to God. *Well, I hope you know I was serious that time. I would have been faithful. Whatever, man, your loss. I was even going to buy your book.*

I always got religious when I was beyond messed-up. I wasn't taught to believe in God, which may be the reason for constantly wanting to taunt him. I was taught about a Creator, but not about the Bible Christian God.

I noticed my bandanna was missing and my jacket was half off. Luckily, the rest of my clothes were on. I wondered if someone from another gang had tried to jack me. I rolled over and saw someone at the end of the bed. When my eyes focused, I saw it was the guy I had been making eye contact with and trying to meet all night.

"You're finally awake. It took quite a while," he said.

My mouth dropped and I was instantly mortified.

"My name is Steve. I didn't mean to startle you, I just wanted to make sure you were going to be okay."

I wondered if he was the one who did this to me. I wondered if Jon brought me in here when I passed out and this guy followed us. But he couldn't have done this to me. Jon was the one feeding me drinks and smoking me up. And this guy stayed to keep and eye on me and make sure I was okay.

"You're probably wondering what's going on, right?" he asked gently, as if he had found a missing girl from a Wal-Mart bulletin board. Before I could answer, he continued, "When I was downstairs I recognized you from another party. I wanted to talk to you but you were with that guy."

"Jon," I spoke quietly in shame.

"Right, umm, definitely not his real name. I noticed he was filling you up with so many drinks. I was watching you because I felt a good thing from our eye contact. But after a while I started to notice he seemed to be up to something."

He took a break, gently giving me only bits of information at a time.

"I was just going to go out for a beer run when I saw you trying to get up. He helped you but I didn't have a good feeling. That's when I followed him here and...as you can see, I stopped him from doing whatever he was planning on doing to you."

I noticed his knuckles were scratched up and his cheek was bruised, and the room was a mess.

"Thank you." I said, still confused. *How could this have happened to me? I was sitting with Jon the whole night–and he seemed so nice and friendly.* I wanted to cry. All of a sudden I felt emotional. I had really thought Jon was my friend. I'd opened up and poured my heart out. I couldn't tell the gang what happened, they'd think I was stupid for putting myself at risk and for not seeing that Jon was trying to pull one over on me.

Steve helped me to a sitting position but I had a hard time trying to sit up straight. The sudden movement made me feel a little sick and I wondered if I should have gone and made myself throw up to feel better again.

"What's your name?"

"I'm Blaise." I answered.

"I couldn't keep my eyes off you all night. I guess it's a good thing, eh?" he said trying to lighten things up. I adjusted my clothes so they were back to normal.

"Don't say anything about this," I fluffed my hair so it seemed messy on purpose. "Please!" I emphasized.

He nodded acceptingly.

I nodded my head in agreement, sealing the deal. I felt my face getting hot with anger, resentment or embarrassment. I didn't want or need to think about which emotion was dominant right then.

"How long have I been out?" I asked.

"About an hour or so," he answered, looking down at his watch.

I got up slowly and headed out of the room, hoping to retain some dignity. He followed me as I made my way down to the basement. I knew he was following me, I could feel it. I picked up speed, fighting against the weakness of my muscles.

"Wait, maybe you should slow down!" I could hear him say from behind me.

I kept moving like I didn't hear him, I didn't want to tell him to fuck off after he'd helped me. But I wanted him to leave so I could pretend it all never happened. I didn't want to live out my moment of shame longer than I had to.

"There you are!" Lindsay said, reaching out her hand, thinking I was really drunk.

"Who's this you brought with you?" she asked.

"Yeah, who's that?" Damion piped up, as he walked up behind her.

"This is…" I looked over to him, and forget his name. *Fuck, I'm such an asshole.*

"I'm Steve." He gave me a half-hearted smile.

Damion looked him up and down before introducing himself. Feeling obligated I turned around and thanked Steve again. While facing him he asked me all sorts of questions that required more than one word answer: "How long you been here? Who all do you know here? Maybe we know the same people?" He was determined to keep up the conversation. Finally I looked him straight in his handsome face and told him what I was really feeling.

"Look, Steve," I whispered in his ear, "under the circumstances, I wanna leave and forget the whole thing. So, if you wanna hang out with me, or look after me, or whatever, then *please* don't say anything about what happened, okay?" His eyebrows came up in his momentary surprise.

"Yeah, I know. We talked about this already, I didn't forget."

I smiled apologetically, feeling like I had said something rude.

"You know, it's just kind of embarrassing right now." I tried to seem more friendly, as I was grateful and I loved the way he looked at me. Maybe there was something worth discovering about a person who can handle seeing you passed out with your mouth open in a starfish position. Although

I didn't want him to know I was in a gang, I couldn't avoid it. I brought him to them anyway, telling him secretly that I wasn't 'really a big part of it'. Usually I thought I was pretty damn cool to be in a gang, but with him it made me feel embarrassingly young. I wanted him to see me like a woman, not some dumb girl with torn hems and no comprehension of moderation.

I tried to pout my lips and sit up straight when he was trying to secretly gaze at me. I felt tickles between my legs when he leaned over to whisper something to me above the music. I loved that Justice had no idea there were sparks flying in front of him. We spent the rest of the night together and I ended up giving him my number. I never had the luxury of someone seeing me at my utmost worst and still thinking I'm worth talking to. I looked forward to seeing him again. I wanted to be dressed up next time I saw him. After tonight, I needed him to see I can look and act like a woman.

By the end of the party I had sobered up completely. I didn't drink or smoke anything else that night. On the way home from the party, I ended up taking care of the drunks in my gang. The entire way home I thought about Steve. I could hear his sexy voice, feel his sweet breath in my ear. Just remembering it sent fireworks throughout my entire core. I was in love with my secret knight.

The next day, I told everyone that Steve might call. Some of them didn't even remember meeting him, but Damion did.

Damion asked me how I met him, and of course I lied. I came up with the most common story I could think of, which was, he was a friend of a friend from school. Justice didn't seem phased by Steve at all. Even though I had hung out with Justice after the party as we planned, he didn't seem to care the next day when I said Steve might call.

When we got home from the party, Justice and I went to a bedroom and shut the door. I let him make out with me even though I really wanted to be with Steve. Part of me wasn't in the mood because of the situation with Jon earlier, but at the same time that was the reason I wanted to. I had full control of this situation and that's what made it alright with me. The song, 'Pretty,' by the Cranberries played on the stereo. It got stuck in my head. The lead singer's chanting lulled me into a comfortable daze. The chorus repeated, "You're so pretty the way you are." It wasn't about the lyrics, it was the lullaby of her voice that got me. While making out with Justice, I kept my mind going from one thought to the next, to the song, then back again. Anything to keep me from being there completely. I needed to feel detached. I was going to lose my virginity.

Justice looked to me with his glossy eyes. He opened his mouth too wide when he kissed me and I grew instantly disgusted and tired. I wanted to want this, but the inside of me didn't really want to. I wanted to start being the girl that was fearless. Backing out would make me feel so young, so I stayed.

After it was over, I went to my usual bedroom and climbed back in my normal sleeping spot with Damion. I fell asleep with my back to him, my lips pink and full from meaningless kisses. I went to sleep with fingerprints as a blanket. Nothing seemed different. Losing my virginity was supposed to be a world-stopping, eye-opening thing, but it wasn't. I was still kind of drunk, I tasted like Justice, who tasted like an ashtray. I knew tomorrow was just another day. I felt cold in a way that was comfortable; I no longer needed the warmth of dependence.

The next day when Steve called, I felt my heart jump and thought of all the cool things I could say to impress him. I was worried he would never call, but now I was worried about making an ass of myself and ruining everything. I knew that he knew I was younger than him, but I was more woman than child now. He had to give me that.

"Hey, Blaise. I called you as soon as I got up. How are you?" he asked, still a little tired.

"I'm fine. You?" I asked, remembering from countless movies and tv shows that it was considered desperate if you called someone the next morning. But he didn't sound worried about it, he actually seemed really relaxed. I was the one who was actually desperate for him.

"I'm good, but I'd be even better if I could see you. What are you doing today?" he asked.

"I don't know. Not much I think."

"Maybe we could meet up? At the theater or something? Maybe just walk around and hang out?"

"I'd like that," I answered shyly.

"Well, can I pick you up? Or are you and W.B. busy today?"

"What?" I asked, a little surprised.

"Your gang, West Bloods, right? I grabbed your bandanna for you; you forgot it."

"Umm, yeah. Thanks. I think we're not doing much. Hold on a second."

I put the phone down and rolled my eyes at myself. Why couldn't I have met him before or after this? Not sure if he was a smoker, and not wanting to ruin our date before it even happened, I lit a cigarette while covering the mouthpiece. I picked up the phone again.

"No, I'm not busy. When do you want to see me?"

He went silent for a few seconds, "I guess after I take a shower and get dressed. I could probably be there by two-thirty."

I told him the address.

"That's far, maybe I'll make that a-quarter-to, okay?" he said.

I knew then that he owned a car, and I was impressed. I wished that I had something as grown up and cool to impress him with. I needed something that told him I was like a responsible adult, like a cell phone that shows up "Blaise Evans" on a call display.

After I hung up the phone, I went straight to the bathroom to shower and do my hair and makeup. Lindsay knocked on the bathroom door while I was applying mascara.

"Hey Blaise, going out with that guy from last night?"

"Yeah. Steve." I smiled at her and asked her how I looked.

"Didn't you hook up with Justice?"

I frowned. "Yeah, but that was nothing. This guy Steve,

he's really hot. Has his own car too," I said slowly while putting the finishing touches on my lipstick.

"Well hopefully you weren't wearing beer goggles. What if he only looked good last night and today you can't stand him?"

Lindsay was bringing me down. I told her I wanted to finish getting ready and suggested she go back to bed and sleep it off a little more. She laughed at me as she left the bathroom.

When Steve rang the doorbell, I answered it, hoping I really didn't have beer goggles on the night before. When I saw him I was delighted. He was still hot, even more so in the light of day. Lindsay came up from behind me and put her arm around my shoulder, "Hey, he's sexy! You really do know how to pick em," she said, chomping her gum loudly. I smiled, embarrassed, and put my shoes on. As I looked back and waved I noticed Justice giving Steve an evil look. I knew he might try to say something threatening so I tried to rush Steve out.

Just then I heard, "Wait a minute!"

My prayer for Justice to just keep his mouth shut failed.

"I just want to tell you now that if she comes back hurt in any way, you can consider yourself dead." Justice finished his warning by trying to issue a frightening stare. I didn't want to make a confrontation when he was liable to say something about last night and ruin everything for me.

"You don't have to worry." Steve told him calmly, unafraid.

Steve took my hand gently, signaling me to leave with him. I let him out first. I didn't know if it was Justice sending me psychic messages, or if it was my own voice I was hearing in my mind, but something kept stabbing the word 'slut' into my back.

# CHAPTER 7

WITHIN THE GANG I CAME to be considered Justice's girlfriend and I was miserable about it. I had to phone Steve and tell him I wasn't allowed to see him again, and that he should move on. We had such a good time together on our date, he wasn't about to give up that easily. He didn't move on. I still snuck around to see him. I never told him the real reason why I couldn't be with him. I lied and told him that the gang made me say that because they felt threatened by him. I was too ashamed to tell him what I had done with Justice, even though Steve wasn't my boyfriend either.

Lindsay was my partner in crime. She followed me everywhere and did whatever I did. Her constant gum chomping, secret-spilling and giggling quickly became a comfort to me. I was bored with Justice before we even began, and Lindsay was growing bored with the one-way streets she called love too.

Damion was a constant disappearing act. He could be away from me and be completely gone. He began doing all the drugs I was afraid to do. When we first moved to the house Damion was as comfortable as a kitten to sleep beside. But he changed with the drugs. He began constantly to feel clammy and he jittered in his sleep. He was beginning to look as dirty and used as the sheets we were sleeping on. I wouldn't try the things he was into. I was afraid of the things I knew I'd have to do to afford them if I got hooked. As naive as everyone thought I was, I was capable of knowing what desperation looked like. It would creep into an addict's belly, soak out onto their skin and eat away every moral they were still trying to standing for. Like weeds that begin to grow from their minds, these drugs wouldn't stop until they reached the back of their eyes and it was all they could see.

I started writing letters to my mother, letters I never intended to send. It was the beginning of June when I wrote to her about how I would have been almost done grade nine by now and how I missed my friends. Later that month I wrote and told her how I wished I was the strong girl I thought I was. How I'd become some loser on the street with nothing better to do with myself then get high and party all the time. How people would stare at me while I was drinking beer in front of McDonalds with Lindsay and give me the, "Where is your mother?" look. Of course I never sent that letter either. In July I wrote to her about how Justice and I got into an argument and he slapped me. How Damion ignored it. How I cried because I felt helpless, and how I was angry because I never thought I'd let it happen to myself. I wanted to write and ask how Sheldon's mom was doing, but I couldn't, even though I didn't plan to send the letter. One day, though, I'd write one that I would be able to send.

The argument with Justice happened one afternoon. I was fuming inside afterward. I hated him, I hated Damion and I hated myself. We fought over some stupid conversation with a mutual friend. He thought I was flirting and I told him he was an asshole. He threatened to make me work the street, and I laughed at him. I laughed in his face and that's when things got out of hand. He did it right in front of everyone but no one even cared, except Lindsay. Damion tried to pretend it never happened and even when I went to cry on his shoulder because I thought he'd protect me, he defended Justice. He said I shouldn't have pushed Justice. He rolled his eyes at me and said, "Come on, Blaise. Get over it." I threw my hands up at him and left the house, saying I wanted to go to the store for something. I saw Damion's jaw clench as he pretended to watch tv. Lindsay followed me, knowing

I was upset. She threw on her five dollar shoes and cheap Hello Kitty purse and trotted after me. Her wrists flicked outward, swinging at her sides. She called out for me to wait up even though I was staring back at her from the end of the walkway.

When we got down the street I went in the direction of the park instead of the store. I really just wanted to get out of the house. As we passed people on the street I hated the way they were looking at me, like I was a homeless person or some street kid. Even though I technically was one I didn't want to see it reflected in a stranger's eyes.

"So why are we going to the park instead of the store?" Lindsay finally said.

"Well, I've been thinking...." I looked back to make sure no one else was around, "I want to run away. Damion's being a jerk and everyone else sucks."

Lindsay burst out laughing. I was confused, *why would she laugh?*

"Of course you want to run away! So do I! But it's not going to happen. We have nowhere to go. No food, no money. Besides, they'll hunt us down! Do you know what will happen to us then? Do you, Blaise?"

She looked at me as if she were expecting an answer. She always made life more dramatic than it was.

"They'll do worse than what Justice wanted to do to you! Remember what *just* happened? He'll beat the shit outta you, Blaise. I know he would."

She continued to laugh, her eyes telling me how naive I was. I wasn't going to take it.

"I'm serious, Lindsay! We can do this. I'm sure that Steve will let us stay with him for awhile. Just until we get jobs and find a cheap apartment. Wouldn't that be awesome to live on our own?"

"And what makes you think Steve would welcome two dirty street kids into his home, huh? What makes you think he won't find me dirty and send me back outside? What will we do then, huh? We would be screwed! No one will take in two gang rats that just finished roaming the streets for the past few months! A few years in my case! Once you start living off the street, there's no going back. Do you know when it's over? When you're dead! Not until then is it over!"

"This isn't real, Lindsay!" I exploded. I couldn't play this game anymore. I couldn't sit there at this moment and play pretend that we were some legit gang.

"It's a bunch of fuckin losers in our gang, Lindsay! Yeah, if we stick around we're gonna get our asses kicked. No argument there! But as for hunting us down? Get real! We're not in some drug dealing ring, we're not even offing people! This is some bullshit gang of street kids. What are they *really* able to do?"

She gave me the same expression I gave her when she didn't want me to answer. I saw her suck in breath to answer me but I didn't want to hear it.

"They won't do shit, that's what. They won't give a shit and in a month they'll forget all about us. Even Damion."

Tears were swelling in her eyes. I wish she hadn't said what she was just about to. "Sheldon's done. You know why? Because he's dead! Is that what you mean by running away? Because there is no running away! You can't run."

A feeling of depression loomed over us. Even though I felt like strangling her, she was really my only friend. I wanted to slap her for bringing up Sheldon. His situation had nothing to do with running away from anything. I sucked my teeth and took out two smokes. Deep in my pocket, I kept Sheldon's switch. Without taking it out of my pocket, I rubbed it in my hand and a lump grew in my throat. After a few awkward minutes she apologized for the low blow about Sheldon. I accepted, of course. We hung out for a while in the park before deciding to head back to the house.

Another week passed before the next party. I broke up with Justice but he wouldn't believe me. He still called me his girlfriend and tried to be normal with me even though I would tell him to leave me alone. On the bus he paid my fair. I didn't say anything. When he sat beside me, I pursed my lips and still didn't say anything. When he put his arm around my seat, then I moved over.

Lindsay and I did the same thing we always do before a party: steal new outfits. Me, Lindsay, Sarah, Damion and a few others all went "shopping." Of course, we had to separate so that the clerks wouldn't be able to keep track of all of us. I noticed clerks were watching me more every time. Things were getting trickier and sometimes I had to leave without anything because I was scared they'd stop me outside the store to check my bags. I hadn't been caught yet, but I'd been stopped.

We ended up at the party around nine or so. I made the prior decision to sneak a call to Steve. I went with Lindsay to a pay phone. Ever since the incident with Justice I wanted revenge and a way out. I knew Steve could fill both quotas. He said he would show up some time throughout the night but he would go with a lot of his friends so that he would have back up if the gang noticed him. I didn't want to make the meeting obvious, so I planned to take off with Lindsay a lot so that when Steve did show up, they wouldn't stalk me so much and I might be able to sneak some time with him.

I was so excited to be seeing him again and to have a chance to better explain the reason for brushing him off. Lindsay was excited too, for Steve and me, but also just to be partying. Like me, she loved wandering off on her own and meeting new people…well *guys*. She loved the way they made her feel sexy just by saying so. Grabbing her ass was a compliment to her. Offering to get her high was the first date. Soon, shame rolled off our backs. I had hated Justice for awhile. He wouldn't take no for an answer anymore either. Sex was how I stuck it to him. After a party he would try to touch me, but little did he knew my skin was protected by the shield of another man's handprint.

The party was the same as any other I'd been going to, loud and disturbing. The people were already wasted by the time we got there. I hated the way Justice constantly tried to put his arm around me or to hold my hand. He was trying to pretend nothing happened, that we weren't fighting anymore. I thought maybe I shouldn't call him any names right now or piss him off because I didn't want a repeat of the other night.

Last thing I needed was a black eye. That would really make adults look at me with that sad expression when I walked down the street.

My decision to avoid confrontation alone made me feel weak and less human. I knew the affection he was giving me was just his way of telling everyone else to stay away from me. He was just being jealous and territorial. I hoped that Steve wouldn't see him touching me when he got there.

We all piled into a small part of the main room and slowly spread our space out bigger. I went straight for the weed; some others went for the booze. It didn't take the gang long to get comfortable and relaxed. I still felt the need to scope out the party before I started roaming. Sometimes girls get crazy and violent when they drink, but they can usually be spotted a mile away. I ended up watching the doorway every time it opened, not to mention I also had my eyes on Justice's watch. I hoped that I wasn't being obvious. When I noticed it was ten-thirty, I took Lindsay by the hand and told her to follow me into the kitchen.

When we got there, we just hung around the keg of beer, trying to figure out how Steve and I could sneak upstairs without Justice noticing. Luckily, the stairs to the bedrooms and bathroom were attached to the dining room, which was right beside the kitchen.

We went up there to see how we could pull this off. We wanted to be ready for the possibility of Justice coming upstairs to look for me or something. I figured maybe we could go into the bathroom, but that was a last resort. That way we'd have a lock, plus I could say I felt sick and then shove Steve into the shower.

I looked around the hallway for any other rooms I could sneak off into. I checked to see which ones were already being used. I felt like giving up. I thought it might not be worth it if I got caught.

"Hey, Blaise?" Lindsay asked quietly.

"Yeah?" I said.

"Ever since I told you how old I am, you've been treating me like a little kid," she said even more quietly. I had to ask her to repeat herself.

"Well, you are. I don't think you should be in this gang at all, especially at the age you are. You should be playing with dolls, not fucking guys."

"No!" She almost yelled.

I looked at her in shock from the volume.

"That's why I told you! I thought you would be my friend. Not my mother!" she whispered hoarsely. She made a good point. She was doing this far longer than she knew me. Why should I feel responsible for her decisions?

"I know. I won't anymore," I said in a quiet voice. I hoped she heard the apology in the tone of voice I was using. I think she did because she nodded her head.

I kept searching the upstairs for a spare room or something. I knew that there were none, but I stilled looked. Lindsay and I walked around the upstairs silently. We could feel the music pulse under our feet. The walls were covered in dainty flower wall paper and antique furniture, like the house had at one point belonged to the classy grandma that wore long white gloves and had a piano in her sunroom. I wanted to make conversation before the silence got to be too awkward.

"Hey, Lindsay. Did you know my birthday's coming up in a week or so now?"

She looked at me, smiling. "What's that now, fifteen?" I nodded my head.

"That's great. When?"

"July 13th." I answered.

"So how long until then?"

"I think ten days or so," I said.

Lindsay nodded her head as she changed the subject, "I don't think we'll find a room. You might just want to stick with the bathroom idea."

"Let's go downstairs to see if he's here yet. I'd rather I found him before Justice or the rest of the gang do," I suggested as I headed for the stairs.

We asked some guy what day it was. Only eleven days until my birthday. I wasn't really that excited though, birthdays weren't as exciting as they used to be. Everyone would just give me money because they'd have no idea what else I'd want. I never complained about getting money though. All I ever had to look forward to were the birthday cards in the mail. My family wasn't organized or close enough to make plans for a birthday.

I sat down beside Damion, only because it was the only spot open. He was too busy making friends to notice me ignoring him. He was smoking a joint with Sara and another girl I'd never seen before. The new girl had wild hair that was shaped like a triangle. Her ends were lighter than her roots and had little white bulbs on the tips of them from being so damaged. The only thing she had going for her were her big breasts. Justice was flirting with her too. I hated his guts but I was still mad at him for flirting. I was even a little thankful for the situation. He had just given me a reason to get pissed at him and storm off. This way I could take off and, knowing him, he wouldn't bother to follow me.

I stared daggers into Justice's back until I spotted Steve. He was smart and picked up on the gang and hid around the corner by the kitchen. I wished I could be with him in the open, mostly because he was actually nineteen and it would make me look older just by standing beside him. This was the time I was waiting for to make a scene. I gave Justice the dirty look to his face.

"What's wrong?" he asked, mildly concerned.

I increased the intensity of my look and shot at him sarcastically as I looked at the girl, "What's wrong?"

"Why don't you two get a fuckin room? Your hand is all over her ass and you think I'm just going to sit here smiling? Waiting for you to come back after your little 'fling' that you just finished right in front of my face?" I yelled.

It didn't matter how loud the yelling was, you couldn't really hear me in the noisy house anyway.

"What are you talking about?" Justice asked, genuinely confused.

"The smart thing to do would be to take your hand off her before playing stupid!" I retorted.

I turned on my heel and stormed out of the living room

and into the kitchen. I motioned for Steve to follow me. We made it upstairs and into the bathroom. I felt nervous and didn't even talk until I was sure Justice wasn't coming.

"I'm sorry about everything that's been happening." I finally said.

"Yeah, I knew something else was up."

I bit my lip before I told him about how Justice had slapped me the other day, after I was told not to be with him.

"That's not right!" he shook his head and after a short pause he said, "do you want me to get someone after him? I will."

I was surprised that he would actually seek revenge over me.

"Why would you get somebody after him?"

"Why wouldn't I?" he asked rhetorically.

"I thought you'd be mad at me for dumping you for Justice," I said quietly.

"Yeah, but you did nothing wrong. He's the one being a bitch."

He got up and walked towards me. I stood up from the floor where I'd planted myself earlier. He put his arms around me and started to kiss me. I reached my tongue in deeper as I thought about him beating up Justice and taking me away with him. The more I thought about it the more I wanted Steve. I started to get paranoid that Justice would all of a sudden bust into the bathroom and see us. But as he started to get passionate with me I melted in his arms and didn't care about Justice anymore. I felt like I was in heaven with him, but I didn't want to have sex. He made me feel so real, but I couldn't make love to him. I didn't want Steve, of all people, to lose respect for me. I knew he wanted me, and was expecting me to want this too. My mom used to always tell me, "If you want a man to stick around, give him something to come back for." My mom was not a guru on keeping men. In fact, she was horrible at it. Even Sheldon and Damion would dump girls if they didn't put out fast enough.

I made a compromise. "Steve, I don't wanna do it in a bathroom. That's dirty." He looked disappointed, but removed his hands from my waist. We sat in the bathroom awkwardly for about ten minutes before we got out, not knowing what to talk about other than Justice or wishing we could have had a bedroom instead of a bathroom. I told him my birthday was coming up, but then regretted that because I didn't want to tell him how young I was.

Steve kept telling the people banging on the door to 'shut the fuck up and wait a minute.' People were already started to build up outside and I felt embarrassed. I almost kicked myself for not looking before I even stepped through the door; instead, I just walked right out into the open! A girl pulled me out of the way and went inside. Steve came out behind me and laughed when he realized one of the people waiting was his friend. Steve still wanted to get Justice back but I told him just to leave it for awhile. I told him he should come downstairs about five minutes after me. He agreed, but he wanted me to walk down with him and tell them all to go to hell and just leave with him and all his friends. He had a great idea, he had a lot of friends there that could defend him and me. Thoughts were racing through my head. I just had too much holding me back, the fact that I came there for Sheldon and I'd promised Damion I'd stay and tough it out, but the romance for those reasons were wearing off now. Now I didn't want to leave Lindsay. I was her best friend. I might be able to convince her to come with me but it would take a lot of convincing.

Now things at my mother's didn't seem so bad. I had only been living with W.B. for about two months or so, but I was getting used to it. I felt a sense of loyalty and I felt safe from the gang that killed Sheldon. *What if it didn't work out between me and Steve? Would he throw me out on my ass?* I'd have to think about it, maybe talk about it with Lindsay and Damion. I'd have a harder time with Damion though. He was right into this gang thing. Why would he pass up friends that gave him drugs for some girl he used to ride bikes with? I really wished Sheldon had never joined this stupid gang! I wouldn't be here if he'd just left the boy alone and walked away from him and the gang. But *no*, he had to prove to them he was tough, and look where it got him!

I was angry and I wanted to just leave with Steve. It just wasn't that easy, though. There was the complication of my friendship with Lindsay. As much as he says it would be, it just wasn't that easy. Steve didn't know about Sheldon, Damion or Lindsay. Those are the people I would have to talk to, I couldn't just leave.

I gave Steve a kiss before I left and he asked to see me on my birthday. I told him I'd try, and if I could make it I'd meet him at the park sometime in the afternoon where he could pick me up. He agreed and asked if by then I could give him a decision about running away with him.

"Yeah, I think so." My heart ached to leave with him.

He nodded his head as I started down the stairs. I wasn't as nervous now that I'd already seen him. I just wished Lindsay was walking with me. I walked up to the gang and they were all staring at me, worried, including Lindsay.

"What's wrong?" I asked.

There was a long pause. I thought that Justice had gotten pissed again and started yelling about selling me again or beating me up. Then finally Lindsay spoke. "We're just surprised that you yelled at Justice. He freaked out and took off somewhere with that girl. I think he just got pissed because you embarrassed him. I don't think he'll try anything, though. He didn't say anything about getting back at you."

I wanted to laugh. I had backup in case my other backup turned on me. Maybe he'd just yell at me a bit and then forget about it. I wished so much just to turn around and run back to Steve and tell him I'd changed my mind. I couldn't until I talked to the people I needed to talk to though. I sighed deeply as I sat down. Just then Steve walked by in the distance. I watched him and he started towards his friends. I saw them start to talk and then I turned my gaze back to the gang who had already changed the subject. I just nodded my head at the things they said to make it seem as if I was paying attention. I was wondering if I should mention it to Lindsay now, or later. She might convince me to leave with him and ask if she could come. That was just wishful thinking and

I knew it. She would have a hard time leaving. I figured it would be better to mention it later.

Justice finally came back. He never said a word to me, but he held my hand tightly and never let go until we got home. As we were leaving I looked back to see Steve one last time. His hair was no longer as perfect as it was before we went into the bathroom.

When we got home, Lindsay, Sarah and I went into the room. Lindsay and I took our time getting ready. We both knew there was a lot to talk about. Sarah, who changed quickly, didn't say that much, and then left the room. I was relieved that we were finally alone.

"Sooo," she started as she turned around to face me. "How'd it go?"

"Well, we made out a bit and he wants to see me again on my birthday," I started.

"Sweet! Are you going?" she asked.

"Well, that's the thing. I'm not done talking."

She gave a confused look and a glimmer in her eye told me to continue. "He wants me to leave the gang and run away with him. He also wants to get someone after Justice."

I stared her in the eye to see how she was taking it before I'd tell her about wanting her to come.

"Oh my God! We gotta warn Justice!" she almost yelled. I stood up in a panic and shushed her, scared that someone heard her.

"Shut up!" I whispered hoarsely. "I don't know if he'll even do it! I told him to leave it for awhile! I just can't afford Justice finding out! I want to do this, I wanted to talk to you first, I want you to come with me."

"What!? Are you crazy? Didn't you join this gang for Sheldon? And what about Damion?!" she shot back.

"Don't you think I know that! I'm done, though. I thought I could do it, but I can't. Sheldon wouldn't want to see me here anyway, and Damion doesn't give a shit what happens to me anymore! I just got to get Damion alone and talk to him, but I really don't like it here and Steve offered me a better place. It's better than always being threatened into things like hooking and it's better then getting slapped around."

"I can't go with you. I support you and Steve falling in love and all that shit. I just don't see why you'd leave us. A gang is supposed to be a family. Are you going to just leave your family?" she asked.

I rolled my eyes, I really wanted to slap her. She took this gang thing way too seriously. Her eyes were all big and twinkling with excitement over the possibility of new drama. She wanted to turn Steve in.

"What do you think I just did for Sheldon by coming here? I just can't handle this anymore. I hate it! I love Sheldon but I just can't do this. Damion can do it on his own. He doesn't need me around. The only reason he took me along was cause he didn't want to do it alone. He's not doing shit and you know it! What's keeping you here? Why are you afraid?" I continued to whisper so Justice wouldn't be able to hear us.

Lindsay didn't say anything else but looked to the ground. I felt bad for saying that, but I didn't regret it. I wanted her to run away with me instead of staying here. I assumed Steve wouldn't mind if I let her come. I was just worried about him using me and then throwing me out on my ass when he was done. I didn't care right now, I just wanted Lindsay and me out of this house. I figured that it would be better on the street than in this hellhole.

I was worried when Lindsay still wasn't talking and I asked her if she was okay. I really didn't want her to rat on me and Steve to Justice. I wondered if she was thinking about it.

"Will you promise me you won't tell anybody about anything that I told you?" I asked. She gave me another pause before she answered, and it worried me all over again.

"I will. I wish you wouldn't do this. You're getting carried away. They'll have your head for pulling this shit. Think about it! Of all the members, you choose to fuck with Justice! He has a lot of pull you know. You won't get away with this one."

I didn't care about what she thought, Justice was an asshole.

"Don't worry about me. As long as you keep your mouth shut about what I'm telling you I'll be fine. Got it?" I said.

"I never thought you, of all people, the new girl, would be yelling at me," she said cockily.

"I'm not yelling, I'm fuckin whispering," I said.

"Whatever. I won't say anything," she said.

I didn't mention that I still wanted an answer from her. I didn't feel like fighting with her. I wished that she'd never told me anything and never trusted me, it would've been so much easier to leave. Damion, on the other hand, wouldn't ever let me get away with this. I knew he said he was my best friend and that I could talk to him about anything, but when it came to loyalties, he could stand anywhere. Maybe I'd just wait for awhile, after I'd seen Steve for a while longer. I'd have a hard time seeing him a lot but it would be worth it. I couldn't wait to see him on my birthday. Maybe something special would happen. Maybe he'd show up with flowers and cake and a little present wrapped in a box. We'd probably end up just making out some more and talk about me running away with him again. Lindsay finally spoke after the second long pause.

"We should go out there."

I agreed, and walked out of the bedroom with her. I stayed close to her until I got to Damion and sat down beside him. I figured that Lindsay would need her space until she had time to think for a bit, and besides, she only wanted to come out to the living room to escape the conversation.

I let Damion pass me a joint. It felt so good to get my mind off things. Damion smiled at me with his huge pupils and I didn't even ask what he was high on besides this joint. I just wanted to enjoy the moment of smiling with him. Then he laughed and looked up at the ceiling, the joint burning in his hand.

"Hey, Blaise?"

I said nothing, just waited for him to continue.

"Did your mom name you that because she likes to get

high?" he laughed more and all I could see was his gaping mouth and bone dry teeth. I laughed too. Him, Sheldon and Tom would always come up with as many crazy reasons as they could for why my mom would choose that name. Mostly the story went that my mom was in a lot of pain after I was born and all she could think about was getting blazed. One time, when me and Sheldon were at my house, he asked her about it. She told him how it was in a baby book and she just liked it. We never told anyone her version because it ruined the fun.

"Hey, remember when we used to stomp on cigarette pack foils on the train tracks and make traffic stop while the gates went down?" he laughed. I did remember. Me and Tom used to do that too, whenever we walked by them.

Justice sat down beside me later on that night and acted like everything was fine between us. I was sort of glad. I just wished he'd dump me or something. I knew he went off to screw that other girl. I was glad I hated him as much as I did. I was pissed off that he would screw that other girl. I wasn't jealous, but it was a slam to me.

"Did you want a drink?" he asked shyly.

"No," I said stubbornly.

"All right," he sighed as he put his arm around me.

I wanted to take his hand and fling it off me and get up. I didn't, though. I wasn't that brave and I was too lazy. No one said much that night, nothing important anyway. The night seemed to go by so slowly. Justice kept trying to get down my pants all night like it would make everything all better. I wished him to hell. When he was drunk he didn't usually take no for an answer. I'd try to push him off when I really wasn't in the mood, but he never let that stop him. He had a reputation to keep. No one said no to Justice.

I hated that little fucker. I hated him with all I had in me, and I had to kiss him every day I spent in this horrible house. Lindsay was still sleeping around with all the guys in the gang, one by one. She did Damion too. It didn't take long to get him in the sack either. I was there when she was all over him and plus she told me how easy he was. I felt like a baby for thinking it, but I wanted to go home and sleep in my own room. I wanted a place where I could shut the door and not worry about who was coming in after me. I fell asleep quickly that night, mostly to help get away from Justice. He came in and touched me under the sheets, trying to wake me up. I played dead hoping he'd give up, but that never does any good. I lay on my back and stared at the ceiling, noticing another water spot I'd never seen before. Concentrating on water stains made time go by faster when Justice was on top of me. I lay there and I could almost pretend nothing was even happening. I almost didn't even feel him. When it was over I rolled over and curled into a ball. I dreamt of nothing.

# CHAPTER 8

WHEN MY BIRTHDAY FINALLY CAME I wasn't surprised that Damion forgot. No one really knew it was my birthday. I didn't care because I knew if I told them it wouldn't really make my day any better. If anything, everyone would try to get me extremely high and way too drunk. But that was normal for me now: hangovers were becoming a part of waking up.

First thing in the morning I went into the kitchen. Justice was making himself a bowl of cereal. He didn't offer to make me any. He reeked of alcohol and morning breath. I was disgusted that he didn't brush his teeth. I wasn't going to say anything though. I'd come to realize things between us were more tolerable when I pretended he didn't exist. I left. I went into the bedroom and grabbed a small notebook and a pencil I still had in my schoolbag and sat on the bed.

*Dear Mom,*

*I hope you aren't mad at me for leaving. I know I should have contacted you earlier (I'm sorry). As you probably know Sheldon died. Did they find out who did it yet? I hope they catch them. It's my birthday today, but I'm sure you haven't forgotten that.*

*I guess you've been on my mind a lot lately. Can you believe I actually miss going to school? I hate it where I am, but I don't want to go home either. I wish there were a way for you to tell me how you're doing and what's going on in your life. I know you're worried about me and you miss me, like any mother would. I miss you*

*too. It feels so weird to know you'll read this. Well, I basically just*
*wanted to tell you that I love you and I'm alive and doing fine...*
   *Love always,*
   *Blaise*

I wanted to see her. Writing her made me miss her even
more. I left the note in the book. I looked around the room
to find something to get my mind off my mother, something
to distract myself from the urge to cry about it. Damion
was still lying in bed, curled up in a fetal position, twitching
occasionally. The lights never bothered him anymore, or
voices. I came up from behind him and crawled in with him.
He didn't move. I tapped him and he flinched.

"Damion, it's me."

He didn't move but didn't protest me cuddling up behind
him. He had gotten a bit skinnier. My face was resting
against his protruding shoulder blade.

Damion teased me about how early I had passed out
the night before as soon as he woke up, trying to poke fun
by saying I was passed out because I couldn't handle my
alcohol. Truth being, I was just tired of the same old useless
existence and went to sleep because I felt alone, ashamed,
and depressed.

Uncomfortable from Damion's twitchy restless sleep, I
got up and went to the living room to grab Lindsay. I quietly
reminded her it was my birthday and that I had plans to go
meet with Steve. I told her I would smoke a joint with her on
the way if she came with me to wait for him. We both waited
in the park for Steve. It didn't take him that long to get there.
Lindsay and Steve said hello and Lindsay tried to keep the
conversation going but eventually things went silent. We all
sat around awkwardly until Lindsay finally said, "I can take
a hint." Before she left, she told me that she'd tell the gang I
found some old friends and wanted to hang out with them
for awhile and that I'd be back in a couple hours. I agreed
with the story and left with Steve in his car.

We drove up to his house. It was a nice neighborhood.
He told me on the car ride he had two younger brothers who

might be home but his parents were out of town visiting family. He didn't say exactly where they were; he said it was personal. Then he got real quiet. I didn't want to press the conversation because I thought maybe someone died and I had no idea how to handle that. I thought of Sheldon and a lump welled up in my throat.

The house had a clean, manicured front lawn. Inside, it was fairly large and very clean. His mom must have been a perfect homemaker kind of wife, unless she had a maid. Steve was very polite. I could tell he was well brought up. He didn't seem like he came from the same kind of dysfunctional family crap like everyone else I knew.

Inside, he showed me the rest of the house. We conveniently ended the tour with his bedroom. I knew he'd do that. I loved his room. It was clean and tidy like the rest of the house. No piles of clothes on the floor; everything was put away neatly. There were stacks with electronics. He had a stereo, a television and a computer on a huge desk, and not to mention, a double bed. His room looked kind of small because of all the things he had in it. I sat down on the bed and he sat down beside me.

"What do you think of my room?" he asked.

"It's cool. I didn't know you owned so much!" I said, eyeing the room for a second time. My mom would never have given me a computer, and my stereo was a cheap little boom box that she got second hand. He looked down at his hands as he talked to me about little things. I noticed him slowly moving his hand closer to mine. I thought he was being so sweet, although it confused me that he was being so shy. He knew I liked him. I made out with him in a bathroom.

I waited for him to take my hand. I could feel this nervous tension in the air. He was obviously feeling timorous so I took his hand in mine and placed it on my lap. He smiled.

"I got you a present." he said.

"Really?" I whispered, my smile shining.

He nodded his head as he got up and went to his

computer desk and opened the drawer. He pulled out a little box of black velvet. I could tell it was for jewelry. I really hoped it wasn't something cheap that he just fit in a fancy box he got from his mom's storage room. He passed it to me and sat back down, a little closer than before.

"I don't know if you'll like it you can give it back if you don't. It won't hurt my feelings or anything," he said.

"I'm gonna like it," I said as I let go of his hand to open the soft velvet box.

I opened it slowly. It was the most beautiful necklace. I had never owned anything that beautiful before. It was a silver chain with a pretty oval pendant covered in little diamond-like stones. I thought it was prettier than anything I could pull off. I was going to have to keep it hidden and stare at it privately.

"This is beautiful," I said. "It looks too expensive."

"Don't worry about things like that." he said.

My heart welled up like never before. I was falling in love with him. I leaned over and gave him a kiss. When he stroked my hair I felt my body heat up in a way that made me want to explode with passion. I laid down and pulled him on top of me. I didn't want to hold back my feelings. I wanted to have sex with him because he made me feel worthy. He wasn't like Justice, who just wanted sex and ownership. We kissed for a long time before he made love to me. It was the first time I really enjoyed myself. I didn't have to imagine anything or keep my mind distracted the way I did with Justice. I did, however, wish that I was wearing lingerie instead of old cotton panties. I never wanted him to let me go. No one had bought me anything like that before. I felt so special. He really loved me. He was everything I wanted, and nothing like Justice.

Unfortunately, I only had a couple hours before I had to go back to the house, so we laid in bed cuddling and we talked for a little while. It was the nicest time I had since I left home. I was relaxed and felt full in my heart. I didn't want to leave, but I knew I had to.

"When are we gonna see each other again?" he asked as he put his pants back on.

I told him I'd try to see him again in three days or else I'd try to call him if there was a party we could go to. He agreed and drove me back to the park. I had put on the necklace to make him happy but knew I'd take it off before I got home. I looked down at it sitting on top of my gray hoodie sweatshirt. It looked like I might have stolen it because it stood out so much against my clothes. My disgusting clothes were seldom washed and worn too much.

He wanted to drive me right to the house to make sure I was okay but I refused instantly. I couldn't let them see him. He understood and let me off a block away. I gave him a kiss before I got out and he reminded me to try to get to the park in three days. I got out of the car still feeling happy and uplifted.

As I started to walk home, I felt so happy! I wished I could tell Damion, but I couldn't. He'd definitely tell Justice. We tried to be best friends but the pretending was becoming too obvious. He was able to have conversations with Fred and Justice, but fell short trying to come up with something in common with me anymore. I was beginning to resent him for never having to be initiated. When I'd ask about it he'd say, "It'll come up," but it never did. I knew it wasn't going to happen. I almost started to skip on the way home because I was so in love. I didn't though. I took the jewelry off my neck and put it in my purse for hiding. It was a good thing I remembered too, because it would've been ripped off my neck and pawned. As I got closer to the house, my happy feeling began to fade. A feeling of doom entered the pit of my stomach. *Why do I have to go back?* I thought as I looked at the house. *I don't want to be here anymore.*

I must have been around 5:30 p.m. when I walked in the house. Justice immediately asked where I was.

"I was with some old friends of mine. Why?" I said, a little snappy.

"Because Lindsay came here alone, that's why!"

"Well, didn't she tell you I was with them?" I asked.

"Yeah, but what if something happened to her on the way home?"

"She's old enough to take care of herself. Besides, she carries a weapon."

He gave me a pissed look and walked into the kitchen. Lindsay shot me a goofy smile that included having her tongue pressed between her teeth and fake excitement. She giggled and I realized she and Damion had been doing something together. They were both laughing and acting silly together. I smiled back.

"Hey you guys, get your shit together. We got some business to take care of," Fred said as he got off the phone. Justice walked out of the kitchen with a handful of dry cereal.

"What business is this?" he asked, as he poured it all into his mouth.

"The Reds are starting shit with us again. Someone just called and told me they were talking shit and calling us out. This is our chance to get them back for what they did to Sheldon," Fred exclaimed. There was a short pause.

"We're doing this for Sheldon!" Fred shouted.

Everyone nodded their heads seriously, especially Damion. This was his chance to do what he was hoping to do when he joined this gang, to get back at The Reds for killing his best friend. I had to fight for him too, and it scared me. I wanted to watch our revenge, not execute it. What if I got hurt or something? What if I died? I started to panic as everyone started to run around getting ready. I followed Lindsay, Damion, Justice and Fred into the bedroom, quickly grabbed my clothes and brought them into the bathroom where I finished getting ready alone. It really didn't make sense that I was putting make up on to fight someone. Maybe I thought if I made myself look pretty enough that no one would want to hurt me. When I was all made up like I was going to a party, I came out of the bathroom and went to the living room.

"You scared?" Damion asked.

"Yes. Why wouldn't I be?" I said.

"This is why we joined the gang. Now we got the chance to get them back! This is what we were waiting for!" He put his hand on my shoulder. "This is what you were waiting for. I was dragged into this for *protection*, remember?" I corrected. "I thought that other gang would come after me for witnessing them killing Sheldon or the cops would think I had something to do with it. You said we were here to keep me safe."

He took his hand off my shoulder and shook his head as if I were ungrateful or didn't want revenge for Sheldon. I was really starting to hate Damion lately. I felt like he no longer understood me. I couldn't wait to get out of here. I wouldn't even mind leaving him behind.

"Screw you!" I said, holding back the urge to push him. Instead, I spun on my heel before he could say anything else and left the house. I decided I would wait outside for everyone, pulling out a cigarette to calm myself. Lindsay came up from behind me and asked to bum a smoke. I took as many deep drags as I could handle and Lindsay tried to support me with her presence. We didn't need to say anything. I didn't want to say anything. Everyone else came out as I was throwing my cigarette butt down.

I walked over to the bus stop. I waited for the bus patiently. It took about twenty minutes before it came. Fred and Damion were the most rowdy of us all. They were constantly trying to pump everyone else up.

"Did you guys know what they were saying? They were saying we're too pussy to show up on their turf, that they come around ours and we don't do shit cause we're bitches. They said that shit."

When we all got on the bus, I grabbed a seat beside an old man because I didn't want Justice to sit beside me. I almost regretted my decision. The man smelled and his hair looked like wet eels hanging from the side of his head. I think he was even surprised someone would sit beside him because he gave me a good look over before staring at the front of the bus again. A few people had to stand because the bus wasn't that big and it was pretty full to begin with. Everyone was fairly silent during the ride. It took us two buses to get there.

The meeting place was a dead end with a fence to block the alley off from what looked like an elementary school. We were the only ones there. I figured they were either really late, set us up, or were here and then got sick of waiting and assumed we'd chickened out. I told the gang what I thought happened. Some of them believed me and the rest didn't think that they would leave so quickly. Just then, I heard a noise from behind me by an old pile of plywood. I whirled around thinking it was a rat or something and I was ready to dart backwards. When I looked down I saw a man's foot instead. He grabbed at me and started to choke me. I tried to scream but couldn't. I heard nothing from the gang. I panicked as the man looked down at me with a smile. He had one of those looks that made me feel like I could have pissed myself. No one ever told me we were at war with a *real* gang. I also didn't understand why they were even meeting us to scrap. I raised my leg and swung my knee into his crotch. I didn't think I'd have the guts to do it, I was so scared. When my knee made contact with him, he let go of my neck and squatted down for a moment. I whipped out my switch and held onto it tightly in case he came after me again. I scuttled backwards as the man started walking towards me again like he was about to laugh.

Damion stood in front of me and in that second I bailed and ran back towards the rest of the gang. Just then I noticed more shadows in the opposite direction. I turned around and there were The Reds with Sam in their hands. One of them started chuckling when he noticed me staring. Sam was crying. He tried to hide it, but his face was scrunching up and turning pink. I noticed a knife under his chin, which was bleeding a bit. I felt like throwing up. These guys were, like, in their mid-twenties and we were just a bunch of teen punks.

"You guys sure picked the wrong guys to fuck around with, didn't you?" the other guy said.

I wondered if The Reds knew that Sam was Fred's younger brother. Fred's anger was melting off him and was replaced with fear. His eyes grew bigger and all the red from built up adrenaline was replaced with white. He didn't know it was so obvious. They sure were lucky to have picked the perfect kid to mess with.

"Get off him you sick fuck!" Paul yelled, looking like he was genuinely sick, shifting his weight from one foot to the other nervously.

All pride was gone. None of us were attacking, we were all deathly quiet. It was like we were watching a balloon grow and grow and all we could do was anticipate the explosion. I felt flashbacks coming, picturing Sheldon's face on Sam's body. I felt dizzy, I looked away, towards the gang. Damion was fighting his jaw from gaping and was clenching his teeth tightly. Lindsay was biting her finger nail nervously, like she was fighting back a whimper. The men behind Sam and his captor started rushing for us. We were defeated. My eyes got bleary when I saw someone looking right at me. They *saw* me. My breathing got heavy and everything slowed down enough for me to float backwards, for my eyes to roll back and see the comforting darkness of the back of my skull.

The next thing I knew, I had a pounding headache and hot liquid on my lips. Lindsay was kneeling beside me asking if I was alright.

"What's happening?"

"Well, besides getting our asses handed to us, nothing," she said. While I had fainted, someone had kicked me in the face and given me a bloody nose. No one else really had a chance to fight. We backed down. The whole Sam incident threw everyone off, and Fred was broken. He wasn't broken in the crying sense, more like you could see he was ashamed of himself and of our gang, like it was the first time he realized we were just a bunch of angry kids looking for recognition, that we were waiting for the moment that the adult world would take us seriously. And at that moment, they were laughing.

# CHAPTER 9

When I woke up the following afternoon, Justice was beside me sleeping. I think it was Justice who woke me because his arm was draped over my body. I slowly took his arm and moved it away from my body, trying not to wake him. I got up and looked around the room. Everyone else was asleep. Sam was sleeping peacefully despite the wound under his chin that was slowly bleeding through the gauze bandage. I got out of bed and went to the bathroom and had a shower. I twisted my hair into a towel and got dressed while still wet. I went into the living room to relax.

"How was your sleep, baby?"

I whirled around, surprised, and saw Justice standing behind me.

"You scared the shit outta me!" I whispered hoarsely.

"Sorry," he said as he put his arms around me again.

I walked to the couch to slide out of his grip. He followed me like a nervous dog and sat down with me. I found the remote on the floor beside the couch and turned the television on. I hated being with Justice in the morning. His breath always smelled rancid. He was acting strangely and clingy ever since our big fight. He was constantly looking me in the eye, searching for any possible admiration. He wasn't able to fight that evening, and that demolished everything he wanted everyone to think he was.

Everyone got up a little later than usual that day, especially Sam.

"I was hoping yesterday was just a bad dream," he said when he got up. I felt bad for him, he probably hated this gang too.

I noticed there was a scratch on Sarah's face. It looked so gross. Nobody mentioned it to her, although I knew everyone noticed. You could tell it wasn't even from a switch. It was just a gouge from a ring or fingernail.

"I'm bored! Let's smoke up or something!" Sam suggested.

"Yeah!" Everyone agreed, looking for something to get the feeling that we were a pack of beaten dogs out of the air. Anything to make the mood less serious.

"Do we got any left here?" Justice asked Fred.

Fred didn't answer, but looked around to see if anyone else had something to share. Nobody said anything.

"Well then, let's go out and get some!" Justice said with enthusiasm.

Fred picked up the phone and dialed the number for his dealer. Justice went around the room with a hat and everyone tossed in whatever money we could use to buy some weed… or whatever we could get. He counted it out on the coffee table. Forty bucks. I knew forty wouldn't be able to get us all high, but Fred said he could get great discounts from this guy he was calling. He managed to get us twice as much for our money as we could have gotten somewhere else.

We rendezvoused at the park for our pick up. I went along with Justice, Lindsay and Fred. Lindsay and I made a playful distraction, laughing and swinging our purses around while they sat on a bench and made the exchange. Everything seemed to happen at the park. It was an oddly depressing looking park, I remembered noticing that from the first time I saw it. The grass wasn't cut as often as it should have been, just like most of the places around here. It was a playground no children should ever be allowed to play in. It was a dirty place where the homeless owned the benches and everything was tagged and empty bottles were hidden everywhere. I'm sure there were piles of dime baggies on the ground near the broken monkey bars.

We ended up smoking up a little of it right there in the park. We went and sat on the old wooden deck at the bottom of the broken down slide. Lindsay and I were in the middle between Fred and Justice, and sometimes they'd switch from clockwise to counter clockwise so the joint passed us by twice as much. They didn't even notice. Lindsay told me that they do that when they get really baked.

When cars would drive by, it used to make me nervous, but not anymore. Nobody cared or bothered us. Unless the cops drove by. But it's easy to see them coming and to clear out. It didn't take us long to get a buzz. Fred told us it was laced, which meant that it had more than just weed in it. I guessed it was crystal meth, because my eyes were burning and so dry and red that every time I blinked it made me blink really hard.

I was getting that dreamy feeling again. When I felt like this I would say anything, and do anything. I had a lot of guts when I was stoned. I wanted to lay down in the middle of everyone and laugh hysterically. I wanted to bang my feet and hands into the wooden structure below me from laughing so hard. I pictured myself doing this, being a childish lunatic, and I laughed. I liked being high. It made me feel invincible at times, or maybe I just wanted to feel that way. Damion and I talked more when we were baked too.

There was only one more day until I could see Steve again. I wanted to see him so bad. I almost told Damion about him during one of our rare moments of comfort. We finally headed back to the house to share the rest of our score.

The next day I went to the park almost as soon as I got up, around eleven a.m. I told everyone I was going to go see a few friends on the street and would be back later. Justice wanted to come at first, probably just to keep an eye on me. Luckily, I talked him into staying home. I reminded him there was still a little weed left from yesterday.

I sat on a swing while I waited for Steve. Kicking the pebbles under me, I reached into my pocket and pulled out the necklace he gave me. I'd found a good hiding spot in the bathroom, under the sink where the empty bottles of cleaning solution were. No one ever cleaned the bathroom or had any reason to look in that cupboard. I took it out and put it on before Steve got there. I rubbed the pendant between my fingers and thumb and the warm feeling from when Steve gave it to me came back to my heart. When I got into the car, he asked me if I'd been waiting long and I said, 'Not at all.' We drove away. He kept one hand on the steering wheel and the other holding my hand.

We kept up our visits and secret meetings in the park for about two months or so before the gang started to suspect something.

"Hey, what ever happened to that Steve guy? You still see him around, right?" Paul asked. *Why was Paul getting nosey in my business now?* He usually kept to himself.

"No. That was a long time ago."

"Yeah, but you must still see him, when you're out wondering on the streets all the time and all," he said as he looked deep into my eyes as if to read through my lies.

"I've never seen him on the streets. I don't think he's that kind of guy." I answered.

"Yeah…sure," he said, with sarcasm in his voice.

"Actually, he owns a car, so why would he be wandering around everywhere?" I was worried that I mentioned that about Steve, especially in front of Justice. They might wonder why I even knew that about Steve. The last thing I needed was for Justice to get suspicious. I was surprised and relieved that Justice didn't seem to react to Paul's comments. I think he wanted him and me to just forget all about Steve. I was surprised that Justice still considered me 'his girl' after four months. He was really starting to believe we had history together.

I didn't want to risk anything between Steve and me, so I didn't see him on the following third day. I waited until six days passed until I went again to our meeting spot. I brought Lindsay too, and took her along in the car. I couldn't afford to send her home alone again. I still saw Steve at parties and such, but I was beginning to worry about the gang finding out.

I was being paranoid like the first time we met up at a party. I was even paranoid at the park lately. I resented Paul for starting suspicions and causing me to feel paranoid. It was because of that stupid asshole that I was acting uncomfortable and obviously nervous. I wasn't able to see Steve as often as I wished.

I occupied myself with other things, like jacking people, doing B & E's, drugs, and a whole bunch of other stuff. I never felt bad for stealing from people, even after seeing their faces in pictures around their houses. I separated myself from guilt by imagining I was Nancy Drew, who was looking for clues and mysteries, except I was looking for particular things to steal. We stole what we could sell. We stole what we needed at the house (even food sometimes). We stole money, clothes, jewelry, and soon I had a good eye to pick out what was worth stealing and what was better left behind.

I noticed my vocabulary changing. It seemed that every other word coming out of my mouth was a swear or some lazy slang. Our gang wore our bandannas less and less often. Morale had plummeted since our brawl with The Reds. In fact, our name was being run through the mud. Any reputation we had was now diminished. We sometimes even referred to ourselves as 'the group' instead of 'the gang.' I was beginning to get used to disappointment. It's all life seemed to offer me.

I started talking to Damion more. Even though he pissed me off, I couldn't afford to lose his friendship. He and Lindsay were all I had. Especially then–I'd been thinking about Sheldon a lot and I'd made the decision to go and visit his grave. I don't know if I needed closure or if I just missed him. I thought we all should go pay our respects. He was a member of this gang and died for (or because of) this gang. I told Damion about my decision first and I asked him to come with me to find Sheldon's grave. His first reaction to my idea ripped at my insides.

"Why bother? It's not like we're actually talkin' to him. He's dead. It's not like we can see him," he said. I couldn't believe it. I felt my toes curl in my socks and my shoulders tense up.

"Well, what? What are we going to do? Ask him, 'How goes it down there?'" Damion said, acting out his words. "He's dead. It'll make no difference to him." He stared at me, then hissed, "It'll make no difference if we show up."

"I thought he was your best friend!" I almost yelled.

"He was! He's dead now. I see no point in going to find his rotten corpse."

My eyes started to swell with water but no tears actually fell. He was high and I was bringing him down. I thought to myself, and wondered if he was just acting like that because of the drugs he was on or because someone in the gang had twisted his thinking. I didn't want to know. I came into this fuckin gang just for Sheldon, and somehow Damion turned it into something else. I made up my mind. I was going to go find Sheldon and then plan out an actual runaway. I'd try to bring Lindsay again but if she wouldn't come I'd leave anyway. I had no purpose here. I was angry. I told the gang that I was going to go find Sheldon's grave and if anyone wanted to come they were welcome to.

The gang fell silent and stared at one another for a response. *Nothing.* I saw Lindsay start to get up but then she fell back deeper into the chair instead. I sighed out loud. I was annoyed. I put on my shoes and a light jacket that I stole from a mouthy girl at the mall a few weeks ago.

I heard a few people say things like, 'I'd go if I weren't so burnt out.' And 'I'll go some other time. A nicer day.' I was so disgusted, I started to open the door when I heard Justice.

"I'll go with you."

At first I was happy that he'd decided to come, until he started to explain why.

"We haven't spent any time together and a walk would be nice."

"What? You want quality time?" I replied, shocked.

"Is that too much to ask?" he said with a little laugh.

"I'm going to see my friend for the first time since he died! I am not your fuckin toy! I'm going to see my friend and if you want to pay respects to *him* then you're welcome too, but don't you dare think of using this as an excuse to 'spend time with me.'"

I waited for a response, but heard nothing– as I had anticipated. I walked out of the house fuming. I bused it to my old neighborhood and I felt paranoid the entire ride there. I kept imagining what I would do if my mom coincidently drove by me or if I saw Sheldon's mom.

When I got off the bus and went to the graveyard, I felt a heaviness in the air that weighed me down. The graveyard had an empty feeling, like a vacant lot in a desolate town. I walked slowly down all the rows, searching for Sheldon's grave stone. It felt so weird to look for my best friend in a graveyard. I checked mostly the newer looking graves, wondering if his would be next, and dreading the moment when I'd find it. It made me upset to walk down the rows, having the sun shining down on my back and the warm wind gently breezing over my body. I was angry at Mother Nature for the nice weather. It was a beautiful day and the fact was I was looking for my dead friend's corpse. I needed sullen and depressing weather. I needed it to be cold and rainy. I needed it to fit. I kept walking until I noticed a grave with Sheldon's picture engraved on it. I walked closer until I was facing the smooth gravestone with my best friend's name written across the surface.

I was upset at first that he was buried. Even though we were just kids, we talked about death. Maybe we were morbid or maybe we had intuition, but I remember Sheldon saying he wanted to be cremated. He said to me, "Just the thought of being dead and rotten in the cold ground makes me want to just fuckin' puke."

We were at the kitchen table at his house. I specifically remembered his mom listening to us while she did the dishes because she said we were being sick and should stop talking about such things. That means she should have known he wanted to be cremated, not buried. I felt so angry. His mom should have respected that wish. I tired to clear my mind.

I took his switch out of my pocket and held it between my hands like someone would a rosary. I kneeled down in the dirt and started to pray. I didn't know the first thing about how to pray, but I tried my best to do it right.

*Hey, um, I hope you're up there. I hope there's life after death, and that you can see me. It'd be nice to know if you can hear me, like, send a message. You can haunt me if you want. Remember when we were kids and we promised each other that if there was such a thing as an afterlife, we would come back to show the other not to worry? Well try your best, okay?*

I said goodbye and apologized for taking off that day he died, and I thanked him because in a way he'd saved my life by throwing me into his house. I read the gravestone aloud to myself.

### IN LOVING MEMORY OF OUR BELOVED SON
SHELDON ANDREW MORRISSEAU
1985-2001

I wanted to have a moment with him, like they always do in the movies. Some sign, like a dove or the wind hitting against me a certain way. I knew it was no use. Damion was right with the, 'he can't answer' part.

I sat down and started to cry. Before I knew it words started pouring out of me. I was talking to him like he was still alive. I told him about running away from home, about being afraid of the other gang because I was a witness to his murder, about being afraid of the cops. I hated my new life. If he was still alive, things would be so different. He never would have allowed all this shit to happen with me and Justice. I told him about Steve and how good I felt with him, about how I wanted to run away from the gang. And how I thought that, really, I'm just a mixed up kid who ended up somewhere I don't belong.

I wiped my face and looked around to make sure no one was watching me. I felt embarrassed for crying, but that was probably a totally normal thing to see in a graveyard, people crying over graves. I got up and left and decided to walk by my mom's house on the way back to the bus stop.

I stopped a block before I got there and pulled out a little note pad and pen from my bag. I started to write:

*Dear mom,*
*I hope you're doing all right. I'm alright. I love you.*
*Blaise*

I folded up the little piece of paper and put it neatly in the mailbox. I noticed there was still another letter in there already. It wasn't a bill. I picked it up curiously and noticed, 'My dearest Blaise,' written on it. I took out the letter and started down the street towards the bus stop. I opened it carefully so I could put the letter back into the envelope when I was done reading it. I guess it just made sense for me to do that. I pulled the letter out of the envelope and started to unfold it. I felt so depressed. I didn't want her to write back. It hurt too much to be reminded of her.

*My dearest Blaise,*
*I hope you are doing fine. I'm just horrible. I miss you terribly and want more than anything for you to come back home. I don't understand why you ran away. Was it me? Sheldon was murdered and you disappeared. I was so scared for what may have happened to you. I thought you might have been killed too. But luckily your friend Tom told me he knew you were alive. I miss you so much, it hurts more than I can say. I didn't touch your room. I've left it the way it was. I'm crying as I write to you. I don't even know if you'll get this. I can't very well mail it to you. I hope and pray you'll find this letter and come home. Please find a way to contact me. I can't stand another day without at least knowing you're all right and why you felt you needed to leave.*

> *I love you so much, Please*
> *come home and we'll face this*
> *together.*
> *Mom*

I started to cry. I wanted to walk into the empty house and just sit there and wait for my mom to come home and see me sitting there. I didn't though. I got on the bus and I went back.

I walked into the house and everyone was watching television, as they always do. I sat down on the floor by Lindsay and thought about everything that'd happened. Nobody said anything to me about Sheldon, and I was glad. I was going to go see Steve today and I almost forgot that was something else that helped me feel better. I got up and got my shoes on again.

"Where you going?" Fred asked.

"I'm going downtown to see if anybody's down there. I don't really feel like watching tv."

"Well, I suggest you take someone with you because you got to be careful."

"Why?" I asked, a little annoyed, but I didn't show it, especially to Fred.

"Because The Reds might be around," he said in a low voice.

I looked over to Lindsay and motioned for her to come, and she did. We both put our shoes on and walked out the door and the gang never said another word. We left the bandannas behind and I left before anyone could mention that Lindsay wasn't really able to protect me from another gang.

"We're going to go see Steve, right?" Lindsay asked.

"Yup."

"I knew it," she said, with a silly smile.

We walked to the park talking about how much we felt sorry for Sam and how Damion was out of line earlier for what he said to me. When we got to the park Steve was already there. He wasn't in the car, though. He was on the swing where I usually wait for him. I walked up to him and asked him how long he was waiting.

"Not long. Hey, Lindsay."

"Hey," she answered.

"I'm going to bring her this time. The gang is getting suspicious."

He didn't seem to mind the idea. He told us to get in the car and we did. We went to his house again. This time, though, his parents were there. They said hello and we did that whole pointless polite chatter and then we all went into his room. I could tell right away they didn't approve of me. I understood. I looked like a homeless person and I was a lot younger than Steve. I wouldn't want my son to date someone like me either. Lindsay left the room not even five minutes after coming in. She wasn't good with adults and probably hadn't been around them for a long time either. If they asked her a question, she always messed up her answers and it made her look like she was covering up her true nature.

Steve's brothers were watching tv in their own room. We all went to Steve's room, but after a minute Lindsay said, "I'll go hang out with your brothers or something," and walked out.

We were left alone in the room at last and we instantly were in each other's arms. I kissed him passionately and we ended up doing it but kept it short because his parents were there. We were in such a hurry we didn't use a condom.

We only stayed for about an hour and then decided to walk home, which was going to take us another hour. I was in such a good mood when I left, but also knew that Lindsay didn't like sitting with his little brothers for too long. I owed her one.

"Hey! Let's go smoke a joint, pretty lady," I said.

Lindsay giggled and we sparked the joint for the long walk home.

"You'd better get that 'just been fucked' look off your face before we get home." Lindsay said, laughing.

"I know, don't worry." I looked to the ground and continued, "I forgot to use a condom."

She looked at me, surprised, her eyebrows raised.

"What? You didn't?"

I shook my head.

"Well, I've done it without one a few times and I never got pregnant or caught anything. I wouldn't worry 'bout it," she said reassuringly.

"Yeah," I laughed, although inside I had a tinge of worry. The weed provided more relief and soon I forgot about it.

We were at the house within the hour. I didn't say

anything when we got there. I just sat down by Damion and zoned out with him. He was always zoned out these days. I tried to find the same piece of carpet he was staring at and thought about all the little dust mites that were sitting there, possibly staring back at me. Damion would occasionally let out a random noise, like he was going to say something but changed his mind. I laughed.

# CHAPTER 10

THERE STOOD STEVE WITH ALL his backup, standing in my front door.

"What do you guys want?" Fred asked, confused and angry. He had a flicker of recognition in his eyes. Steve looked past him at me while he pushed his way through the door.

"What happened to you!? Did you get into a bad fight?" he asked, concerned.

"What the fuck do you fuckers think you're doing?" Fred yelled.

Justice looked angry and he pushed Steve away from me.

"No, these fuckin W. B. pricks did this to me!" I almost screamed.

I was overwhelmed with so much fear and nervousness, I felt like I couldn't even breathe. As soon as Steve was in sight of everyone, with a huge group of men behind him, I knew what was going to happen. The men were, or at least seemed to be, much bigger than us. A commotion was starting and everyone was getting their defenses up. I noticed that two of Steve's friends were wearing blue bandanas tied to their arms. I felt my eyes widen when I finally put two and two together. Steve was down with The Reds and I just made the biggest betrayal of my life. Everyone else soon recognized their colors and maybe even their faces. It was too late to turn back. I was either going to be killed or I was going to walk out of this house with The Reds.

"Hey, what the fuck?" Damion asked me, confused.

The intruders were standing all around the surprised, outnumbered gang.

"What's going on here?" Fred asked nervously.

They said nothing and just stood there.

"Look, you guys," Fred started, nervousness pouring from his words.

"We don't wanna do nothing to you. We deserve the same, you know. We just want to go have a good time."

"Shut up and go outside you fucking bitch! Beatin' the shit outta little girls. You're gonna learn something today, boy," the taller man said.

"What?" Fred repeated. "I don't beat up no girls. This is all a big misunderstanding!"

"Then what's the matter with her? She fall down some stairs or some shit?" the tall man said sarcastically, pointing to me.

"She just got into a fight! Isn't that right, Blaise?" Fred asked, giving me a pleading look.

"Fuck you! You lying piece of shit!" I yelled.

He dived for me and I shot back against the wall.

"You little bitch!" he screamed.

Steve ran after Fred and that's what started the fight. The whole thing didn't take that long. Some of the W. B. didn't even bother to fight. Fred got it pretty bad. I watched and felt like crying and Lindsay stood there in disbelief. Fred kept yelling, "Just take her!" Steve grabbed my arm and jerked me out of the house.

"Lindsay!" I screamed.

She said nothing. I don't even think she heard me. She just stood there, looking at her friends and all the ruckus going on in the small house. "Lindsay!" I screamed desperately.

I was already outside by that time, and Steve told me to hurry up. I felt like I was a complete traitorer. Even I hated me.

We all squished into a dark blue van and I didn't say a word. I tried to disappear into the corner, hoping to get sucked in and not be noticed. I knew that I didn't fit in, and I also knew that they knew it too. I kept real quiet and only spoke when I was spoken to. I didn't even want to remind them I was there. I felt embarrassed to have a group of strangers see me like this and rescue me from some stupid teen gang. I wished then that I could have been strong enough to do it on my own.

"So what really happened to you?" Steve asked.

"I told Fred to fuck off and he got mad and slapped me. Then I got mad and hit him back. That's what started our fight and I ended up clocking him with an eight ball and everyone else beat me up for it too."

"You okay?" Steve asked.

"Fine." I answered.

"Don't have to be so shy, girl," one of them said.

I smiled weakly. I wanted to be polite but couldn't start a conversation. I was sitting with the wrong people. They killed people, they were serious, and they'd been known to shoot people. Like, actually carry a gun. No words could describe what was going through my head, the nervousness and fear I was feeling by being in the hands of complete strangers. They killed Sheldon. I knew I was dealing with people who were much stronger than all those guys in that house. I knew because the fight was already over and no one had come outside to stop us.

They spoke of the same things that W. B. did. They sounded exactly like them. They made the same kind of jokes and the same kind of discrimination. Steve sat by me the whole time and I was thankful, but I had to find a way to leave.

"Where are we going?" I asked.

"To my friend's house, then to my place."

I nodded my head.

"You'll like him, he's a nice guy. He gets a lot of respect round here."

When we made it to his friend's house, I was even more

nervous. Now they expected me to go to one of their houses? I knew I asked for it, and I actually did. 'Steve, help me get out of this,' I said. I remembered saying it and I shouldn't have been sorry for it. Steve kept his arm around me when we walked into the house. It was a small comfort. Not that many people were there, just four guys playing cards.

"You guys in?" the fat man said as we entered, not even turning around to look at us.

"No, maybe later." Steve said, as we started walking towards the couch.

"Who's the girl?" the fat man asked, finally noticing us.

As I looked up at him to introduce myself, my mouth dropped. He looked familiar from the beginning, but it was then that I realized this was Sheldon's murderer. I didn't know what to do. What could I do? Turn and run? What if he had seen me that day and he knew I was a witness, or what if he heard I was a witness from other people? Tom and his big mouth might have told my story to people. I tried to hide my nervousness. *Did he know who I was?*

"Your name?" the fat man pressed on.

"Blaise," I answered quietly.

I kept my head down lower than before and sat down beside Steve. I wanted to run off a cliff and die. I was in the killer's house! On his couch! Telling him my name! The other two guys weren't there. I was thankful for that one tiny thing. It would be just as bad if they were all there. I was a traitor. How could this have happened? How could I not have known they were friends? Steve had caught on to my continuous nervousness because within fifteen minutes of us being there he asked where his car was.

"It's in the garage. I used it to go to the store. Hope you don't mind?" the fat man asked.

"No problem, man," Steve said as he took the keys from the fat guy and motioned for me to follow him to the back door. We sat in the car for a while as he fiddled around.

"That ass messed it all up," he explained, readjusting the seat and mirrors.

"What's the matter? You're acting weird," Steve said.

I didn't say anything. I didn't know what to say. How would I explain it without lying? The fat guy's name was Shawn. He had no reaction when he looked at me. If he recognized me, I'm sure I would have noticed. I was pretty sure I was safe, but my heart was still racing.

"You nervous around all these new people? Tired?" He kept pressing, "I'll get the shower ready for you when we get to my place. You stink." he teased.

"Thank you," I said, trying not to laugh, unaware of how I should feel about Steve.

"Do you want to tell me what's wrong? You never answered."

"I'm … nothing's wrong." I stammered. He frowned and started the car. Maybe I'd tell him at his place. I couldn't right now, I was still wishing the fat man wasn't who he seemed to be. If I told Steve about Sheldon he'd know that Sheldon was the one who killed that guy. Since that guy and the fat man belonged to The Reds then I was sure that Steve knew I was a witness.

Steve went into the bathroom and put up a new towel since I told him I really did want to have a shower. I stood in the shower, letting the water pour down my back. I stood there longer than I needed to, thinking. I wondered what the gang was doing, or thinking. I wondered how Damion and Lindsay were doing. I wondered if I should get someone to call there and ask for Lindsay. I knew they'd recognize my voice. I didn't know what to do. Maybe if I waited three days and go to the park, Lindsay would be waiting there for me. I wondered for a long time about everything. I got out of the shower and dried myself off. For the first time in my life, a towel was a luxury.

"Feel better?" he asked as I walked out.

"Yes." I answered.

"Tired?"

"Yeah."

We went into his room to lie down, looking at the ceiling again. I was surprised that he never pressured me more about the way I was acting tonight, as I was sure he would. We just talked about all the other things that were bothering me, like the gang, Damion and Lindsay.

The next morning was full of questions, questions like what were we going to do when his parents came back. We talked about all the different options and there weren't very many.

"Well, I'll try to get a raise at my job, or else look for one that pays more. Until I make enough to get us our own place, you can stay with my buddy Shawn, all right?" Steve offered.

"Who's Shawn?" I asked.

"The fat guy." he answered, laughing.

My eyes widened. This wasn't good at all. Steve noticed my expression.

"Well, I know it doesn't look like the best place to stay, but it's shelter, you know?" Steve defended.

"I know, I know, it's no problem." I said.

I didn't understand what I was saying, but I couldn't risk being found by W.B. and I felt like the biggest scumbag for agreeing to stay with the fat man. I also realized there wasn't much lower I could go in anyone's books that I'd pissed off. All I had left was Steve. I didn't want to offend him.

Three days had passed in Shawn's house. He tried really hard to be friendly to me, but I only talked to him when I had to or when it was polite. I couldn't help but realize that I was in his house and eating his food and I didn't know what else to do.

We were alone one day, so I asked him to call Lindsay for me.

"Is Lindsay there?" he asked.

"They said she's there," Shawn told me. "They told me to hang on," he said. A couple seconds later he passed me the phone "Hello?" a voice asked.

"Hey," I said quietly.

"Hi." Lindsay said a little surprised.

"I got someone else to ask for you. You want to meet up today?" I asked.

"Mmmm," Lindsay started.

"I know you can't say much without giving it all away, so just say yes or no. Don't say anything else. Okay?" I explained.

"Yeah."

"Yeah to what?"

"Both." she replied.

"Okay, I'll see you at the park in half an hour?" I asked.

"Sure." she whimpered.

"What's the matter?" I asked.

"I'll be there." Lindsay reassured me, but she sounded odd.

I couldn't understand what just happened. Did they have call display? Do they know where I am? Did they know who I was with? What if they all came to the park knowing I'd be there? Maybe I was overreacting, Lindsay wouldn't do that, but I knew Damion would. She deserved to hate me.

"Hey, Shawn?" I asked, initiating conversation for the first time.

"Yeah?"

"Do you think she'll bring W. B. with her?"

"I've got no idea." he replied. I got off the couch with a sigh and went to the door to grab my shoes.

"Well, did you want me to go with you to make sure?" he offered.

"Please." I said.

Shawn had some buddies staying with him. He borrowed a car and we headed out.

I didn't really like this idea, but at least I was safe, and it was better than taking the bus.

We made it to the park on time, and nobody was there.

"She running late?" he asked.

"Probably." I hoped.

I couldn't stand to think she was too mad at me to come and see me. We were waiting there for about fifteen minutes. Shawn was watching me sit on the swing before Lindsay showed up. The closest bench was at an awkward distance for keeping company with me.

"Hey, who's that?" she asked as she approached us.

"Oh this is Steve's friend, Shawn. I'm staying with him for awhile. He's the guy that asked for you on the phone," I explained. I felt like I was lying to her by not letting her know who he really was, but, really, there was no other choice.

"Oh." she said.

"I guess I'll head home now." he said as he started to get up.

"Oh, okay." I answered. "Thanks for waiting with me." I added.

"All right. I'll see you later. You remember how to get back?"

"Sure do," I answered. He left and Lindsay and me were alone.

"So how have you been?" I asked, trying to get the conversation going.

"I'm okay I guess," she replied. "I wish you didn't do that."

"Do what? Leave? Or the whole thing with those guys coming over? Because I had nothing to do with that. I was just as surprised as you were."

"Both." she said.

"I'm sorry. I didn't mean for it to get out of hand like that. I didn't know that was going to happen," I apologized.

"Fred is real mad, so are Damion and Justice," she said.

"I can understand why they feel that way. I still don't want to talk to them, though."

"Well what about Damion? Don't you owe him an explanation? You guys were friends for so long," she added.

"Yeah, until he pulled all that shit! He pulled me back into the house and helped them beat me up! Why would a friend do that?" I almost yelled.

"You don't understand!" she said.

"What do you mean? You saw what he did!" I screamed.

"You're being a self-centered little bitch!" Lindsay screamed over me. I looked at her in surprise.

"He did it to keep you safe! He thought he was protecting you! He was teaching you a valuable lesson and you can't even see that! He was trying to keep you with him because he loves you like his sister and you're too blinded by Steve to see it!" she screamed and started to storm off.

"Wait!" I yelled, and ran after her.

"Let go of me!" she screamed, as I grabbed her arm.

"What's the matter?" I asked in disbelief.

"You've changed! I thought you joined us for Sheldon!

Now you're off with some other gang!"

I let go of her and let the tears stream down my face. Hiding them would only make me look more guilty.

"The Reds," she repeated as I stood there crying. "You should cry!" she screamed.

"I'm sorry! What do you want me to do?" I yelled in frustration.

"Talk to Damion!"

"He'll hurt me!" I whimpered as I tried to dry my eyes.

"Give him a chance!" Lindsay said, a little calmer.

"Only if you're there! Promise me you'll be there!" I asked, also calming down.

"I promise. I'll go get him, okay?"

"No! What if the gang finds out?" I panicked.

"They already know!" she said.

"What? How could you?!" I started screaming again.

"Well, they put it on speaker and I couldn't do anything. They'd be so mad. You understand that, right? And they didn't come here, did they?" she said.

I looked around the empty park, too nervous to move.

"I'll go get Damion," she said again.

"Let's just phone him from the payphone. I don't want to be left alone!" I begged.

"Got a quarter?" she asked.

I handed her a quarter and we called the house. I could only hear the one side of the conversation.

"Yeah, she's still with me."

"Let me talk to Damion."

"Yeah, she's here. She wants to talk to you."

"Yeah, but only you."

"Yeah, see you in a bit."

"Park, yeah."

"Bye." And she hung up.

I didn't need to ask what he was saying. All I knew was that Damion was on his way here now and I was ready to piss my pants.

"What do you think will happen?" I asked nervously.

"Nothing," she said.

We waited in the park for about another half-hour before Damion came. I held my breath and thought about all the things he might say to me and all the things I could say back.

"Long time no see," he said as he came closer.

"Yeah, I know," I answered quietly.

I was sitting on the swing and as Damion stood right in front of me, he stared down into my eyes. The wind made his jacket ruffle around him. It was the black jacket I wore so many times. My hair blew around my face.

After a few minutes of silence I was too afraid to break, he finally asked, "Were you that mad? To leave your friends? To leave Sheldon?"

I let myself cry in shame once again - I hated myself.

"I know," I whimpered.

"And for The Reds at that?" he rubbed in.

"I know, I know," I cried, and let my eyes focus on the ground. There was more silence. I could hear my own heart thump against my ribs and I could hear Damion's slow steady breath.

"Look at me," he said. I did, and it made me feel so little.

"I miss you. We don't hate you. You're still young, and that's why you weren't allowed around that gang when Sheldon was still around. I felt bad for bringing you there in the first place. I wish I'd let you stay at home."

"I'm sorry," I cried. "I'm so sorry."

"Come back."

"No, I can't now." I said immediately.

"Then promise me something?" he asked.

I raised an eyebrow.

"Promise you'll come see me and Lindsay, if not at the house, then here at this park?"

"Okay."

"So you'll come to the house?" he asked with hope.

"No, never. I'll be at the park." I answered.

"When?"

"I've got no plans this week," I said.

"Tomorrow," he said. I nodded. He hugged me goodbye and I hugged Lindsay.

I walked home and had a smoke. I'd been rolling them at Shawn's house. I'd never rolled cigarettes before, but I was good at it. I was so relieved after I talked to Damion. Everything that happened before seemed like nothing now. I forgot how much he actually liked me.

I made it to the house in time to play a game of poker with Shawn and his friends Rick and Gary. I won a couple games and I actually had fun. I didn't mean to. I had met one of the other guys from the murder only yesterday. His name was Ryan. He was the taller one. I still hadn't met the other one. Rick was a funny guy and he had a lot of respect. I couldn't picture him as a murderer. I just couldn't see it in him. Gary wasn't actually in The Reds. He was just a friend and their drug dealer. I never did do drugs with them. That was something I only did with people I trusted. I didn't want to ever trust these people. I had to keep in mind what they did to my best friend. I tried telling myself that I was planted here as a spy, to learn everything about them and then to plot my revenge.

"When is Steve going to come by?" I asked.

I haven't seen him since I first got to Shawn's. Shawn looked up from his cards and answered.

"I dunno, call him," he said.

I got up and walked to the phone, dialed the number, and let it ring.

"I don't think he's answering," I said to Shawn.

"Then hang up," he answered, laughing. He had a really low voice that took a while to understand. He was constantly breathing hard like he just jogged down the street.

I let them laugh and hung up the receiver and decided to try again later. I really wanted to see him.

I didn't want to have too much fun with these guys, knowing about Sheldon. I still wondered about what was going to happen tomorrow with Damion. Was he going to keep begging me to go back with him? Or just call me a traitor? I had no idea what was going to happen and it frustrated me. Our meeting went too well. He should have yelled at me. It made staying here seem less of a big deal and

I wasn't okay with letting myself off the hook that easily. But what if Justice tried to come tomorrow? Would Lindsay have the guts to say otherwise? I was so worried and I wanted Steve with me so bad. I had no one to sit with or gossip with. I needed a best friend.

I looked at the clock and realized it was almost 11:30 at night. I just wanted to fall asleep and forget all about this. I wanted to ring Steve again I but wasn't sure if I should.

"Okay, I think I'll go to bed now," I said as I started to get off the couch.

"Why so early?" Gary asked.

"I don't know, I just want to sleep." I lied. Really, I just wanted to be alone.

"You haven't had any fun since you came back," Shawn commented.

"Hey, if the lady needs her sleep, let her sleep," Rick said.

"No, shut up Rick," Gary commanded.

"Stay up for a bit and chill with us. You never talk to us. We too ugly for you?" Gary joked.

"I talk," I said.

"Yeah, right. Why don't you tell us how the hell you fell for Steve?" Gary asked, trying to keep up the conversation. I laughed a little and shrugged.

I knew that they were all stoned, but I just didn't want to be rude. That's the only reason I talked to them.

I started off by telling them about me being in W. B. and how I was never in the whole street thing before that. I made sure not to mention the murder or my seeing them doing it. I mentioned Damion slightly but couldn't say much without mentioning Sheldon. I never realized until then how little of a life I really had.

# CHAPTER 11

I woke up to the sound of Shawn in the kitchen. "Want eggs?" he asked.

"Yeah!" Gary answered. Gary was always around.

I crawled out of bed and went into the living room. For the first night in a long time I had my own bedroom with my own bed. I sat down on the couch beside Gary.

"When are you going to go see your friends?" he asked.

"Later, not until about three or so," I answered.

Shawn served up some eggs. He offered me some, but I wasn't hungry. Shawn's house was bigger than the one I came from. It was actually close to the size of my mom's house. It was definitely a bachelor pad. The bathroom was totally empty of any decoration and the living room was covered with florescent beer labels and signed pictures of naked girls in frames. I didn't want to sit there and listen to them chewing their food so I excused myself to take a shower. When I came back out I noticed that no one saved me any eggs. I had grown accustomed to Justice always having food waiting for me. I guess I should have grabbed a plate even though I wasn't hungry at the time. I took a piece of toast off the counter and went back to the couch, where Gary and Shawn were sitting.

"What are you guys watching?" I asked as I sat on the old rocking chair.

"I dunno yet," Shawn said. "Just channel surfing."

"I think I'll go to the park alone this time." I said, more to myself than anyone else.

"Are you sure?" Shawn asked.

"Yeah, I think it'll be better this way," I said, determined.

I sat around the house and waited for three o' clock to come around. I felt I could trust Damion and Lindsay. They wouldn't hurt me, not intentionally anyway.

When the time hit exactly three I put on my shoes and jacket and started out the door. I felt so defiled being in that house. I shouldn't even have been there. I should prefer to be dead than live with that murderer. Guilt hung over my head like a black cloud. I walked faster, hoping I'd get there before Damion and Lindsay. Maybe that way I could see them before they'd see me. Then I'd know for sure if they brought anyone else. I came around the corner and poked my head out behind the fence. They were already there on the swings. I spun around the corner and started to walk towards them. Lindsay was the first to notice me, and she nudged Damion and cocked her head towards me. He stood up and started to meet me half way.

"Hey," he said, as he grabbed me and pulled me into his arms. A feeling of awkwardness overcame me. He hadn't hugged me for over three months. I could see Lindsay over his shoulder. She stared at me intensely and darted her eyes from me to the street and back. I looked towards the street but couldn't see anything. I looked back at her, confused, using my hands to ask, 'What are you talking about?' She repeated the action and I became nervous. My stomach knotted and felt heavy. Damion was still holding me, still making me feel awkward and now I was afraid for myself. Lindsay slowly brushed her jacket to reveal a switch in her pocket. I was so confused, and Damion still held on to me. They couldn't be betraying me. *Damion wouldn't do that. He's not that crazy*, I tried to convince myself. Lindsay looked like she was going crazy herself over there, but I didn't know what to make of her signals. I noticed her jaw clutch in frustration. I looked over to the street again and could still see nothing. I tried to look around the street but nothing seemed out of place. I knew something was happening, but what was she trying to tell me? Was she telling me to run from them in that direction, or escape it?

"I think you can let go now, Damion," I said, as I patted his back.

"I'm sorry, you know," he said.

"I know, Damion. I am too, but let's go." I said.

He started to tremble a bit and I knew he was getting pumped for something.

I tried to pull away but he didn't let me.

"Damion, you're freaking me out. Let me go," I started.

He squeezed harder and I felt a breath escape me.

"Let me go!" I yelled.

He covered my mouth with his hand and pressed against my face hard then turned around to face Lindsay and nodded. Lindsay got up off the swing and started towards the sidewalk. I fought harder and tried everything to get out of his grip. I started screaming, whimpering and crying. I couldn't help it. But Damion's hand muffled everything that was trying to get out of me. Lindsay waved at someone and started to come back. She was looking behind her the whole time. She walked towards us slowly, not at all phased by what was happening to me. I kicked Damion in the balls. He fell but still held on. I pulled my leg out from the tangled mess he became.

I saw Justice and Fred coming fast towards me, but my legs already started to run. I ran and it burned. I was screaming so loud that I made my own ears ring.

"Fuck off!" I kept pleading to the mob behind me.

I had about six people running behind me. I couldn't see them all, but I knew that Damion was one of them. I was so close to Shawn's but I couldn't go in. I couldn't take the chance of them knowing where I was staying. My plan was to keep screaming as I soared by the house. I hoped this would get their attention and they would help me. I was really close now; the house was a block or two away. I pumped my legs harder as my hair was already starting to stick to the sweat on the back of my neck. It felt like my lungs were caving in and someone had thrown a flaming torch down my throat. I darted passed the first few houses and screamed Steve's name as loud as I could. My heart was pounding, my breath was burning and my legs seemed to be turning into Jell-O.

"STEVE!" I yelled, "Help me!" No one answered.

"For the love of God! Somebody help me!" I screeched. I had no idea what they were planning to do when they caught me. I had never been so afraid for my life.

Just then, Shawn ran out of his house along with another small man. They pulled out a gun and I stopped dead in my tracks, lunging forward, barely catching my steps. I could hear the gangs' footsteps slow down, but I still stayed glued to the ground. Damion came crashing into me and I fell on my face right down to the pavement with Damion on my back holding me down.

He held me down and I heard more steps and a shot.

"Fuck!" Damion screamed over the shot.

They shot again and it was so loud.

"Please let me go," I pleaded.

Another shot went off.

Lindsay and the gang who had been chasing me took off in all directions away from Shawn and Steve. The only ones left were Damion and I tangled on the ground.

"I'm not letting you go until they drop their guns," he said, tears streaming down his face.

"Drop your guns!" he yelled.

His face was on my shoulder and his tears soaked my shirt. His grip on my arm was too strong and I could feel him pulling it back harder.

"Fuck you!" he muttered into my back. I could feel my shoulder begin to pop as he kept pulling it farther behind my back.

"You're hurting me!" I screamed.

"Fuck you, Blaise. Tell them to leave," he said, as he yanked my arm. I could smell alcohol on his breath.

"Damien, you're drunk. Think about this," I pleaded again. I knew he was on something else and didn't want to ask. I wanted to be able to talk him down, but I knew at this point he was gone. My arm was straining in a way that was unforgettable. I pounded my fist into the ground, trying to tap out. A shot soon followed my scream and some blood splattered on my neck and hair. Damien rolled off of my back and onto the road beside me.

"Damien!" I screamed.

He stared up at me, shocked.

I started to cry and he just stared at me, angry and in shock. I looked at his shoulder where the blood was coming from. He followed my eyes to where he was shot, and stared at it blankly.

He grabbed my arm. "Look at what you've done, Blaise."

I heard, felt, and saw nothing. It felt like I wasn't even there. For a moment, I felt like I would open my eyes and I'd be sitting there with Damien and Sheldon, eating pudding and listening to shitty music.

"Are you going to be okay?" I whispered.

No response was given. "Damien?" I asked again.

He was on his back with his eyes closed and asked me to leave. The gang was already gone and blood was everywhere. A car came screeching up to us and inside it was Gary, Steve, and Shawn.

"Get in!" Steve yelled.

"I can't just leave him here," I said.

"Get away from me, Blaise," Damien said hatefully.

I couldn't stand him hating me, although I knew it was getting to that point.

"Come on, Blaise. Let's go," Shawn said, and tried to grab my hand.

"Fuck off!" I yelled. "Just fuck off!"

Shawn grabbed me and Steve sat me down in the car.

"Don't touch me!" I screamed, "You fucking murderers! Don't ever touch me!"

They said nothing and drove to Steve's house.

"Come on, Blaise. Let's go inside." Steve said calmly as we pulled into the driveway. It was the fastest car ride I've ever had. All I could think about was how much farther we were getting from Damien. How he was lying there, sobering up, alone…and hating me.

I said nothing, did nothing. I just sat there. I was alone, all alone. I wanted to go home, to go back in time. Steve grabbed me out of the car and hugged me. I walked into the house with him hovering over me. My shoulder began to hurt, a lot. It throbbed and it felt like all the blood that was supposed to be pumping into it was just floating around lost and taking up too much space.

"I need to go back," I said.

"You can't. People are probably there already," Steve explained.

"I need to call the cops or something," I panicked.

"No, you can't, Blaise. Shawn will get in shit for that. He was doing it for you. You can't turn around and rat him out."

He started going towards the living room, expecting me to follow. I don't really understand why I did it, but I turned quickly on my heel and went back out the door. He yelled for me and I heard him begin to come after me. I started to run and I heard him stop at the end of the driveway.

"Don't tell anyone, Blaise!" He yelled to me.

I trotted down to walking when I was a couple houses away. I think he was still at the end of his driveway, watching me.

I ended up walking for awhile. I went past the mall, towards my old school, by old friends' houses, by the graveyard, but I never stopped anywhere. I knew all the places I couldn't go but I couldn't find a place where I belonged. I smoked almost the whole time, until my throat was dry and phlegm. Now I was feeling homeless and thirsty.

My legs were still sore from running when I came across another park. This park had children and slides and parents. I trotted over to a tree off in the corner of the small park and leaned on it. Listening to the kids playing and conversations of those who sat in earshot, I soon found a nice spot beside a tree that looked like a good place to rest. I leaned against the tree and slowly lowered myself to the ground, wincing as my thigh muscles stretched and burned. I pulled my knees into my chest and sat with my chin on my knees, my left arm hanging limply to my side. I saw that my jeans had gotten ripped at some point today, probably when I got smashed into the road. There was blood inside my jeans, but my knee was already scabbed. I realized after noticing everyone around me, that I looked like shit. I had blood on me, dirt on me, sweat, and I had dirty, knotty hair. I'm not sure how my face looked, but I'm pretty sure I was no prize. Realizing I had no chance of seeming graceful or proper, I laid down and shut my eyes to take a nap. *They think I'm homeless.*

# CHAPTER 12

THE COOL EVENING BREEZE WOKE me up and as I got off the grass, every muscle in my body was stiff. I stretched, not really processing anything, but enjoying that part of waking up when you think maybe you were dreaming. But reality quickly surfaced from the pain in my shoulder. I walked out of the park, wondering where I should go. I wanted to see Lindsay. I wanted to make sure she was okay. Going to the house wasn't an option after everything that had happened.

I walked around for a while. I headed downtown, walking and thinking about everything that had happened since Sheldon died. I stopped at a payphone and made the bold decision that I didn't care what they thought. I was going to phone the house and check on Lindsay. It's not like they could hurt me over the phone…right?

Justice answered and I told him flat out, "Hey, it's me, Blaise."

"What do you want?" he asked in an angry voice.

"Lindsay" I uttered.

"What? Speak up!" he yelled.

"Lindsay!" I yelled back.

The phone went quiet, then finally I heard, "You got nerve calling here, bitch."

"Where is she?" I repeated.

"Try the hospital," he said, and slammed the phone down.

"Fuck," I whispered to myself.

I wasn't surprised. I sighed as I walked to the bus stop. I knew they did this because she didn't come after me. All that faking didn't help her at all. They knew she was warning me the whole time, and then they made her pay. I took the bus to the nearest hospital where I thought she'd be. It was in the same neighborhood as the house.

"I'd like to know if someone's here?" I asked the woman at the desk.

"What's the name?" she asked, ready to type into her computer.

"Lindsay Conner," I answered.

I could hear the clicking of the keys of the board. I felt numb, and nothing could help that.

"Are you related to her?" she asked.

"No, I'm her friend and she'd want to see me."

She pulled out a sheet that had a map of the hospital printed on it. She had a highlighter in the other hand and began drawing me directions to her room. I followed the map in the hospital maze, and found her room.

Lindsay was sitting up in the bed watching the television with no sound. She didn't notice me at first. I walked into the room, feeling horribly guilty and trying to show it.

She looked over to me, a bit surprised to see me there.

"Blaise, what're you doing here?"

As she turned to face me I was taken aback a bit by her face. It was bruised up and she had an eye she couldn't see out of because it was so swollen. She didn't, however, look like she needed to be in the hospital.

"I wanted to see how you were doing. I'm sorry," I said.

She pursed her lips into a smirk that implied, 'Whatever, bitch.'

An uncomfortable silence filled the room, and the moment lasted forever. I didn't know what else to say. I thought I'd come in here and everything would still be the way it was with us, but things had changed drastically. It was as if I was in a room with a total stranger. I could tell Lindsay felt the same way. She had a look that seemed like she was constantly on the verge of saying something, but then changed her mind.

"Umm, so have you heard anything from Justice?" I asked.

She glared at me for a second, and I held my breath, feeling like a complete asshole.

"No, have you?" she asked sarcastically.

"I said I was sorry. I don't know what else I can say. I didn't know any of this was going to happen and I'm sorry it did. Why didn't you just leave with me when you had the chance?"

She didn't react the way I thought she would. I thought she would have gotten really mad at me for saying it. Instead, she calmly asked me, "Did it ever occur to you that maybe I didn't want to leave?"

I made an exaggerated expression of surprise.

"Uhhh, no! You said you wanted out as much as I did, remember? How would you expect me to translate that into, 'No, it's okay, you go on without me.' What the fuck Lindsay?" I was so frustrated.

She looked right at me and said, "I was your friend. I wanted to support you, but I never planned on leaving and you know it. I bent over backwards trying to help you out because you were my best friend! Now everything I've ever done to prove myself to them and myself is gone! I have nothing. The hospital and the cops said they're gonna try and get me in a group home now."

I wanted to pull my hair out and scream, but instead I just sat there, expressionless.

"So what do you want to do now?" I asked.

"I'm not sure, really," she said, completely calm.

"How long do you think they'll keep you here?"

"Tomorrow morning. They just want to keep me overnight."

"Why are you even here? Were you hurt that bad?" I asked.

"No, not even. I was knocked out and when I woke up some guy was helping me up and insisted on calling the police. So I waited there with him until they came and got me and brought me here."

Lindsay adjusted her pillow as she told me how she was worried about me.

"I was fine. Damion got shot, though."

Lindsay's eyes widened with worry.

"Is he dead?" she asked.

"No…I don't think so. The bullet was in his shoulder and he was still conscious and pretty pissed off."

"So he might be in here too, then," She said.

"Yeah, probably."

"Are you going to check?" she asked.

"No, I don't think so. You can ask, but I don't think we'll ever be able to talk again," I said.

She nodded her head and stared at the silent tv screen again.

"So, are we still best friends?" I asked.

"Yeah," she said, without taking her eyes off the screen.

I knew she didn't mean it, and she was just saying it to make me feel better, or to keep us from having another awkward conversation. I knew she was done with me, that we would never be the same.

"Well, I'll write down a number for you to get a hold of me, and my address," I said, taking the pen and paper beside the phone.

"Sounds good," she said curiously.

"I should get going. I got some people to see," I lied.

"For sure… hey," she called out to me.

I turned around to face her again.

"Are you going back home?" she asked.

I nodded my head yes, and she turned back to the television, dismissing me. I turned and left the room, knowing that was likely our goodbye and that she may never call me. I realized that every time I've said goodbye to someone it was never the way I'd thought it would go. Things always seemed too normal, or too angry. Goodbyes with me were never happy endings to great stories.

I got off the bus a block early to give myself some more time to think about what I was going to say my mom. I didn't come up with anything. It was weird. For so long I wanted to go home, but I was just dreading seeing her. I knew I would be in trouble, and I knew that there might be a long night of talking ahead of me. My mom was pretty hit and miss about things like this. I was hoping she'd just hug me and say how happy she was to see me. Maybe feed me some real supper, and tell me how my room was still the way I left it.

I walked up to the front door and stopped. I sighed, my heartbeat beginning to race, and I could feel thumping in my throat. I hoped to myself that my mom would swing the door open and get it over with, but she had no idea I was standing there. It was up to me to open the door and show myself after months of hiding. I closed my eyes and reached my hand out to the doorknob. I grabbed it, and counted to three, held my breath and opened the door. I stood in the doorway and lightly shut the door behind me. Nothing seemed different. I kicked off my shoes silently and debated whether or not I should call out to my mom. I climbed up the stairs and no one was in the living room. I went into the kitchen, where I saw my mom reading a book and smoking a cigarette.

"Hey mom." I said.

She looked up at me, startled.

"Holy shit, you scared me!" she said, as she put her hand to her chest.

"Sorry."

She got up off her chair and hugged me. It felt really good. Usually our hugs were awkward, but this time it felt like we meant it. We spent the rest of the afternoon talking about what I had done, what I was doing, and what I'd better start doing now. I got grounded and on the one hand I was upset she'd do that. Did she not listen to me talk about how grown up I'd become because of this? On the other hand, I felt relived to be home and to know someone else was responsible for me again. When I asked about Sheldon's case, she told me I she hadn't heard anything yet.

I went down into my room, which as far I knew, wasn't messed with. I could hear my mom on the phone, telling everyone I was home now, grounded, and asking if anyone was going to need a babysitter in the next few weeks. I laid on my bed and thought to myself, 'What if I go back to school, and Damion comes to get back at me? What if Tom starts spreading a bunch of bad rumors about me? How much did I actually care?' I noticed a picture of me, Tom, Damion, and Sheldon sitting in my backyard for a barbecue tacked up on my wall. We were sitting in a semi-circle of lawn chairs, eating corn on the cob because we were too hungry to wait for the burgers and steaks to finish. Damion didn't notice the camera, and Sheldon was smiling for my mom behind the lens. Tom stuck his tongue out and crossed his eyes while I made an exaggerated smile. I took the picture down and stared at it, smiling. I brought it over to a framed picture I had of my old dog, Bud. I switched the pictures, putting Bud on my dresser until I had time to find a new frame. I placed the newly framed picture on my nightstand. Everything worth mourning needed a frame…always–like it would disintegrate if not preserved between cardboard and glass.

My mom had picked up all the piles of paper and binders that I'd left on the floor that day and stacked it on the nightstand. On top sat the, "My life as a movie," project. I picked it up and began writing the missing entry, knowing full well that my teacher would never accept a project this late.

*Author photo: Courtesy of Stephanie JM Photography*

Jennifer Storm is Ojibway from Couchiching First Nation in North Western Ontario. Born and raised in Winnipeg, Manitoba, Jennifer completed this first novel *Deadly Loyalties* at the age of fourteen. In 2006 Jennifer received the Manitoba Aboriginal Youth Achievement Award as well as the Helen Betty Osbourne Award. Jennifer is currently completing her second year of Native Studies at the University of Manitoba in Winnipeg.

Printed in November 2007
at Gauvin Press, Gatineau, Québec